# Then I Met You

Janet Koops

Brown House Books

Book Cover by: 100 Covers

Print edition: May 2024
ISBN (paperback): 978-1-963745-03-0
ISBN (ebook): 979-8-9865521-8-7

# Books in the Lost and Found Family Series

Homing Instinct
Six Weeks With You
Rules of Disengagement
Family Friends
Then I Met You


**For a complete list of all of Janet's books, please scan the QR code or visit janetkoops.com**

For Derek, Emily, Graham, Melissa, and Kodi.

# 1

OF COURSE, IT HAD to rain. Avoiding puddles as I made my way to Isabelle's car proved challenging, and my suede boots were a poor choice. Still, they were comfortable and sexy, and tonight, I needed to look my best. It wasn't every day—make that ever—that I had tickets for an art exhibit on opening night.

"Wow, you look amazing," Isabelle said as I slid into my seat.

"Thanks. I clean up okay, and there's enough hairspray on my head to survive a hurricane." Isabelle and I worked at an art store. She was the manager, and I was the only other full-time employee, although we had several art students working part-time. Our daily attire was casual, and this was the first time either of us had seen one another so dressed up. "You'll have to let me know what you think of my dress. I took a chance at the thrift store. It's got a seventies vibe with oranges and browns."

"That's a lovely fall pallet," she replied. "Perfect for the season."

"That's what I thought, too. And you don't look too shabby yourself," I said, noticing her refined outfit.

Isabelle nodded as she pulled onto the slick road and into traffic. "I own one dress, and this is it. You know me, I'd rather be in jeans and a T-shirt any day."

"Don't forget about your Union Jack Docs."

"Don't tempt me. They're in the trunk in case my feet hurt."

"Well, if anyone can pull off a little black dress and Docs, it's you."

"Thank you, my friend," Isabelle said. "Now, let's get going. I'm excited to see Oliver's work. He's been in the store so much recently that I was wondering if we should start paying him. Of course, I'm not sure it was the art supplies he was after." She turned to me and wiggled her eyebrows.

"We're friends. Nothing's happened between us."

"So?"

"So what?"

"Maybe tonight's the night. My guess is that he didn't want any distractions while he was finishing up his collection, but now that he has his show, things can progress. Wink. Wink. Maybe you can offer to do some nude modeling for him. You're sure he never had you take your clothes off?"

"Positive, considering it was outside and in March. Not only would I have been arrested for indecent exposure, I'd have been rushed to the hospital with hypothermia."

Isabelle laughed. "And you've never seen the painting?"

"Nope. He's very secretive when creating."

"You artists are a funny bunch."

"I'm not an artist. Not like Oliver is, anyway."

"What do you mean? I've seen some of your work, and you have three sketches in that bar."

I stared at the passing cars as we weaved through the dark streets toward Old Montreal, remembering the rush when the bar owner wanted several of my sketches. Perhaps that's why I enjoyed spending time with Oliver. His dedication and hard work inspired me to focus on my portfolio again. I'd stopped, content with working at the art store. But Oliver's energy proved contagious, and I hoped tonight would inspire me all the more because I was struggling to create anything meaningful.

The sketches I sold originated from a very dark place, and that part of me had mostly healed. So, while I continued to draw, I did it for fun, not as an emotional outlet. That needed to change if I was going to have any success. "My sketches are like posters, whereas Oliver creates art," I told Isabelle.

"You said you haven't seen his work."

"I haven't, but I can tell. Besides, this show is proof of that."

"I hope you're right. I don't wear a dress unless it's important," she said, making us both laugh. Then, a song came on the radio, and Isabelle began to sing along.

We approached the neighborhood where the gallery was located, so I scanned the street for parking. "There's a spot," I said suddenly, causing Isabelle to slam on the brakes and park the car.

"Perfect," she said. "Only a block from the gallery, and the rain has stopped." She turned off the car and handed me the keys. "Are you sure you don't mind being the designated driver? I don't plan on getting wasted, but I'm not going to turn down free drinks."

"Not at all. You know I don't drink."

"But if things go well with Oliver..."

I rolled my eyes, and we laughed again while hurrying to the gallery, having left our coats in the car. The cold air stung my skin but cleared my mind. Yes, I liked Oliver, but I didn't want anything to happen. Harmless flirting was enough. He wasn't...he couldn't compare to...Daniel. No one could.

The lights from the gallery lit the sidewalk like a red carpet, drawing us in. Gallery Etoiles took up the first floor of an old historic building with floor-to-ceiling windows facing the cobblestone street. The door was wedged open, unsurprisingly, because as we stepped inside, the heat from the lights hit like a wall. Soft jazz, humming conversation, and expensive perfume filled the air. An exposed stone wall faced us on the left, while the remaining were perfectly smooth and white. My teenage artistic dreams paled compared to this reality, and I passed the doorman our tickets while engulfed in awe. Isabelle pulled me over to the bar and ordered a glass of white wine for herself and a club soda for me.

"It's busier than I expected," Isabelle said.

"Yeah, I imagine Oliver is thrilled."

We scanned the room for him before Isabelle gently elbowed me and tilted her head to the left. And there he was, surrounded by a small crowd. A tall, thin, stunning woman with white-blond hair and cornflower eyes introduced him to the group. Her posture radiated confidence while her hand gestures flowed like a song. I couldn't hear her voice, but her audience stood captivated. Who was this siren?

"Oh wow," Isabelle said. "That is Celeste Deborough, the gallery owner. She comes from family money, if it wasn't obvious. And she always looks amazing. Oliver looks pretty good, too, though."

"He does." Instead of old jeans and sweatshirts covered in a rainbow of paint streaks, Oliver wore a black suit atop a black shirt. He'd slicked back his fine blond hair that, combined with the harsh light of the track lighting, emphasized his sharp Anglo-Saxon features, reminding me of the chiseled features preferred during the early Classical period. He usually resembled the stereotype of the absent-minded professor. This was an Oliver I'd never seen before.

"I thought he was a starving artist. That suit costs more than my car," Isabelle whispered.

"Do you think Celeste bought it for him? Is that typical, or do you think they're...together?"

"Hard to say. He'd want to look good tonight, so I imagine he'd buy something new. But wow. That is one heck of an expensive suit." As soon as the words left her mouth, Celeste linked her arm through his, and he leaned over and kissed her cheek. "Okay, maybe there's a chance they're together. Let's go over and find out."

"Not yet. I want to look around first." While I admired Isabelle's direct approach, I wasn't ready to talk to Oliver without first seeing his work.

We approached a series of small images painted on wooden blocks, ranging in size in both depth and width, although they were all perfectly square. Each block had a car part on it: headlights, wheels, grill, and so forth. This three-dimensional floor-to-ceiling collage, entitled Congestion, was the first in his Modernity series. It left me feeling crowded and claustrophobic, which I assume was the point. Oliver was off to a good start.

I'd moved on to a painting of a twelve-lane highway piercing farmland when Isabelle gasped.

"You said you didn't pose naked," she said, tugging on my arm.

"I didn't." But as I turned around, I saw myself painted that way. My naked form sat perched on the lookout wall at the top of Mount Royal, gazing out across the city. In reality, I'd been wearing jeans and a wool sweater, my knees drawn up and my arms hugging them against my chest. But Oliver had painted me naked. As the painting wasn't of me, per se, his creative license didn't bother me. My expression, however, did. The only word to describe it was longing, and when I noticed the title was precisely that, I felt a little woozy.

When he'd suggested posing there, up on Mount Royal, I'd resisted. The place brimmed with memories of Daniel, so much so that I called it 'our spot,' and the thought of sitting there, lost in recollections, while someone's gaze dissected my form for their painting was unimaginable. But Oliver had insisted, and I agreed, not wanting to reveal my baggage to him. As it turned out, I did anyway. He'd not only seen me, he'd seen right through me. Painting a nude form made complete sense as I'd exposed myself that afternoon.

"Vic, he's coming," Isabelle whispered, gently placing her hand under my chin and closing my gaping mouth.

He strode across the room, his smile as wide as the nearby St. Lawrence River. "Vicki, Isabelle, thank you so much for coming tonight." He leaned in and kissed us both on each cheek. "Your unwavering support means the world to me."

"You're very welcome," Isabelle said. I remained silent, still too shocked to find words.

He faced me. "So what do you think–"

"Oliver," interrupted a large man, slapping Oliver on the back.

"Marco, how brilliant to see you and Antonia here tonight," Oliver's voice boomed with newfound confidence. He shook the man's hand and gave the woman a kiss on each cheek. "Let me introduce you to Vicki and Isabelle. I don't normally reveal this, but since we're all standing here, I have to tell you that Vicki is my model in Longing." He gave me a wink. "The one that Celeste thought would appeal to you."

I smiled awkwardly while Antonia scrutinized my face before focusing on the painting. "Ah, yes," she said. "How wonderful for you to be part of Oliver's vision. What does it feel like to be included in the collection of one of the best up-and-coming artists in the country?"

My mouth went dry. Usually, I talk when I'm nervous, but knowing these people enjoyed gazing at my heartache caused my mind to go blank. I took a sip of water as she awaited an answer. "I don't know what to say," I admitted.

"I know. It's incredible." Antonia reached across and squeezed my arm.

"It's certainly something."

"Oh, darling, look over there. It's the Rutherfords. Let's go say hello," Marco said, placing his hand on the small of her back. He turned to Oliver. "We'll be in touch."

"I look forward to it," said Oliver. Marco and Antonia walked away, leaving us in a cloud of Chanel Number 5.

"So, what do you think?" he asked me. "I know you didn't pose nude, but there was something so vulnerable about you up there; I knew what I had to do."

"I completely understand. So how—"

"Ah, there you are, darling," Celeste Deborough interrupted as she floated over to us. "And who do we have here?"

"This is Isabelle and Vicki. They are my lifeline to art supplies."

"How wonderful," Celeste said, giving us both a smile before turning to me. "You must be the Vicki who posed for Longing, no? Oliver said his model worked at the art store." She flicked her hair behind her shoulder, barely waiting for me to nod my head before saying, "Now come, darling, you simply must meet the Wheatons." We'd been dismissed as unimportant, or more specifically, unwealthy.

Oliver gave us a small bow, then followed Celeste across the room. Isabelle looked at me, eyebrows raised. "Looks like Oliver has a patron."

"You could say that."

"Do you think she knows you didn't pose nude for him?"

"Maybe, but if she doubts his word, I can show her my tattoos. He didn't paint those."

Isabelle laughed and linked her arm with mine. "Come on, I need more wine."

I took one last look at the painting as we walked away. Something about the muted grays bothered me. Or was it the dullness in my eyes? The epiphany hit suddenly, causing me to stop short.

"Are you okay?" Isabelle asked.

"Yeah. Sorry. I just...Oh, never mind. Let's get you that drink." We continued toward the bar, discussing the other guests' fashion choices, and I was relieved Isabelle didn't ask what had caused me to stop. The epiphany had been profound. The longing that Oliver had captured was only a fraction of who I was. Oliver had missed the vibrancy Daniel infused into my life. The love, the confidence, the joy. Since Daniel, I'd made friends I considered family, had a cute apartment, a dog I adored, and a fantastic job. A life that had been charcoal gray was now a pallet full of colors. Yes, I missed Daniel, but even without him, my life remained rich and complete. And while Oliver's drive and focus inspired me, I now knew I didn't need this measure of success to be fulfilled. Not only that, my art, once a refuge for my intense emotions and a lifeline through my darkest times, had evolved. I simply enjoyed using my talent to bring joy to the people I cared about. My life was beautiful the way it was. I didn't need to advance my career. In fact, I didn't need to change anything at all.

# 2

As I opened the front door, a strong fall wind blew leaves into the foyer, creating an autumn rainbow of pumpkin, burnt orange, goldenrod, maize, saffron, and amber. Breathing deeply, I filled my lungs with the crisp, earthy air and warmed my cheeks in the low fall sun. It was a perfect fall day.

Perfect for moving, especially since it wasn't me. I loved my tiny apartment and never wanted to leave. Situated on the first floor of an old row house that had been converted into three apartments of varying sizes, mine was the smallest. But I had no complaints. The building was clean and warm and close to the metro. And it got better still. What was once simply a place to live had become a home full of friends. And that number was about to grow.

As I secured the door open, I heard scratching at the window and turned to find Gunner, my dog, peering out and tapping a paw against the glass. "Don't worry," I called out in an effort to comfort him. "I won't be long." Of course, he would indeed worry. After being abandoned in an empty apartment, he feared being left behind. I was fortunate enough to be able to take him to work with me, so he wasn't alone often. And he could do it when necessary, but it required plenty of reassurance. No matter how many times I proved my love, always returning, he could never shake that deep insecurity.

Before he could guilt me into opening my apartment door, I ran up the stairs, calling out a hello as I entered Matt's apartment.

"In here," Jenna said from the kitchen. "Would you like a cup of coffee?"

"I'd love some. Thanks." Matt's apartment was perhaps five or six times bigger than mine. Maybe even more since it spanned two floors. Considering Jenna and her daughter Abby were moving in with Matt, they needed the space.

"I'm happy to report that my apartment is empty," Jenna said. "We've been moving things over for the last few days, and as you know, I didn't have much to begin with, so it was pretty easy. And Josh and Sylvanna are keeping the couch, so we didn't have to move that beast, which is a relief. Remember the struggle to get it in there in the first place?"

"I sure do." Matt moved in the same day as Jenna, and his couch became wedged in the hallway. Unable to fit it through his door, they moved it into Jenna's apartment and traded couches. That was how they met.

Jenna handed me a coffee, and we both sat at the kitchen table. "I can't believe this is happening," she said. "And I have you to thank for it. I know I've said it before, but your friendship changed my life. You told me about the apartment, helped me start my business, and didn't give up on me when I fell apart. Now, I'm moving in with Matt and have reconnected with my sister. It's unbelievable."

Emotion clogged my throat. I didn't consider my behavior special. All I did was tell her that my building had a vacant apartment because Stephanie moved out.

"I know Steph and I tease you about being a magical unicorn," Jenna continued, "but honestly, you are the glue that binds us all together. No, more than that, you are the sun at the center of our universe." Her voice wavered. At least I wasn't the only one getting choked up. "I'm sorry. I didn't mean to get all emotional, and I hope I didn't make you uncomfortable. I just want you to know how much you mean to me." Jenna laughed and shook her head. "Listen to me. I'm moving across the hall, not heading off to war."

Jenna's words went straight to my heart, but I was one of many, hardly an anchor point. "I know what you mean, but it's not just me. We all play our role in this crazy group of friends." It was true. I loved everyone in this building since I first ran into Stephanie on the stairs. Both she and Jenna had become the sisters I never had. And that family continued to grow, including Jake, Stephanie's boyfriend, and Matt, who moved in across from Jenna. "And now it's bigger with Josh and Sylvanna. Speaking of which, should we be worried about how much stuff they have? That apartment will be a tight fit for two people."

"No kidding, but Josh wants to be close to Abby, and Sylvanna is supporting that decision. He's a lucky guy."

"Abby must be excited, but what about you? I know you and Josh get along, but isn't it weird to have him move in across the hall?"

"Yeah, it's super weird, but also a good decision. Surely, by now, you and Steph are tired of me talking about it." Jenna shrugged. "Life is weird. All I know is that the best way forward means letting go of the past."

"You should put that on an inspirational poster," I teased.

Jenna stuck her tongue out at me. "Hilarious."

We both turned toward the door as heavy footsteps stomped up the stairs.

"We're here," Josh called out.

Abby burst out of her room and flung herself into Josh's arms. "Daddy! Daddy! Daddy!"

"Hey, kiddo," Josh said, lifting Abby into his arms before turning to Jenna and me. "Morning, ladies. Any more coffee?"

"Help yourself," Jenna said, tilting her head toward the coffeemaker.

Josh balanced Abby on his hip, then poured coffee into a mug with his free hand. "Well, the good news is that this shouldn't take too long. Sylvanna's brothers are here to help, and she did an amazing job of..." he paused, searching for words, "culling our inventory. She should forget about costume design and focus on home organization. The woman's ruthless."

Jenna and I laughed.

"I should have her come to the art store," I said. "My boss never wants to get rid of anything. Our storage room is a mess. How much will she charge per hour?"

"What's Josh telling you?" Sylvanna asked as she strolled into the apartment. She stood beside Josh and planted a kiss on Abby's cheek.

"Just how wonderful you are," Josh said as she took his coffee and had a sip. "Where's Matt?"

"He went to buy some donuts and stuff. We're not that organized this morning," Jenna replied.

"Sorry, I was out last night, or I would have done some baking," I said.

"Who cares about baking? How was your hot date?" Stephanie asked as she walked into the apartment, and all eyes turned to me.

"Sorry to disappoint you all, but it wasn't a date. It was two friends going to an art show."

"Yeah, right," scoffed Stephanie.

"It was. I went with Isabelle, my boss."

"Yeah, but you knew the artist. You modeled for him," Stephanie continued.

"You mean the artist whose girlfriend is Celeste Deborough? Yeah. He's interested in little old me." Playing along was easier than justifying my lack of interest in dating anyone for the umpteenth time.

"Celeste Deborough has nothing on you."

"Except for a family fortune, an art gallery, and a supermodel's body."

"Well, besides that," said Jenna.

"Enough tormenting Vicki. Let's get this show on the road," Sylvanna said.

"Yes, Mom," Stephanie said playfully, then held out a hand to me. I grabbed it, and she pulled me out of the chair. Stephanie let the others walk ahead of us, then said, "I thought there was potential with this guy. You talked about him all the time."

"I know, but it was professional infatuation and harmless flirting, that's all." I sighed, causing her to put an arm around me and squeeze.

"So, he wasn't the right one. You'll meet someone when the time is right."

"I guess," I shrugged. "But it's not like I need someone."

"I know."

Steph was placating me. Because she was madly in love with Jake, she struggled to accept that I was happy alone. No matter how many times I explained Daniel was the love of my life and no one could replace him, she continued to pressure me about meeting someone new, albeit in a friendly, loving way. Her intentions were good, but I didn't need love. I'd had that, and no new relationship could compete with all I'd shared with Daniel. The thing was, and I'd never admit this to Stephanie, that I longed for another single person to join our group because being the only one who wasn't in a couple occasionally left me feeling like the odd man out.

# 3

A FEW DAYS LATER, I returned home from work with Gunner at my side to find Abby in the hall playing with Poppet, Matt's Shih Tzu. Poppet yipped at Gunner, who barked excitedly in response. I barely managed to unclip his leash as he raced toward Poppet and Abby.

"How was your day, Abs?" She was sitting on the floor with a tennis ball in her hand.

"Good. We're playing ball tag. Matty's making dinner because Momma has a new client, and Daddy's still at school. Sylvanna's having dinner with her mom. Did you want to have dinner with us when Momma gets home?" There were no secrets when Abby was around.

"Another time. I have some cookies to ice, and then I'm going to bed because I'm exhausted. But thank you for the invitation."

"Okay. Can Gunner play with us?"

"I think he is already," I said, watching Gunner, who not so deftly tried to take the ball out of Abby's hand.

After unlocking my door, I left it open so Abby and her doggy entourage could come in if they wanted. As I hung up my coat, I noticed my smiling reflection. I loved this house, and how much my life had changed since I moved here continually amazed me. I was alone and afraid those first few months, refusing to get a phone in case Kent, my ex, found me.

Now, I belonged to something bigger, and Kent was no longer a factor in my life.

As soon as I kicked off my shoes, I put the kettle on for tea. Walking home from the store had taken an hour, and I was chilled to the bone, but it had given me time to think about the final designs on the cookies I needed to ice.

While my tea steeped, I pulled out the ingredients for royal icing and mixed them together. Something about the rhythmic motion of stirring, the hum of the mixer, and the soft scraping of the spatula against the bowl always anchored me in the present, distracting me from the constant whirl of thoughts in my head. And the artist in me loved watching the pure white base take on any hue I could imagine. The entire process of creating something beautiful from such base ingredients provided me with a profound sense of peace. What can I say? It served as this poor girl's therapy.

Sipping some chamomile tea, I decided on a pale green for the base layer, as the cookies were for a baby announcement and were shaped like a onesie. Once completed, I called Gunner in for dinner and reheated some spaghetti for myself. Gunner finished eating and jumped onto the futon for a nap. I cleared my dishes and mixed more icing in varying shades of brown, orange, and gray. In the center of half of the cookies, I crafted a puppy; on the other half, I crafted a kitten. I was completing my last cookie when there was a knock, and my door opened.

"Hello, hello," Stephanie called out in a sing-song voice as she walked in to be greeted by Gunner, who rolled onto his back for a belly rub. "What are you up to?" she asked while squatting down to appease my dog.

"The usual. Decorating cookies. But I'm finished. Just let me wipe my hands." I washed them in the kitchen sink and set the bowls to soak. "What's up?"

"Notice anything different about me?" Stephanie twirled.

I attempted to spot something new. "Um, your shirt?"

Stephanie scoffed, then wiggled the fingers on her left hand.

"Oh, my gosh. Is that...are you engaged?"

"Hell yeah, we are," Stephanie said.

I wrapped her in a big hug, squeezing her tight. "I'm so happy for you both."

"Thank you," she said, withdrawing from my embrace. "It almost doesn't seem real. I mean, it shouldn't be too surprising since we live together, and things are great, but wow. This is it. We're getting married."

Stephanie collapsed onto the couch, and I sat at my table with a glass of water. "So, when's the big day?"

"We're not exactly sure, but likely next month."

I nearly spat out the water I'd just sipped. "What?"

"I know. And no, I'm not pregnant. We simply thought, why wait?"

"But is that enough time to plan your dream wedding?"

Stephanie pat Gunner, who'd curled up beside her. "I know I've talked about big fancy weddings, but it's not what I want." She spun the ring on her finger. "A few years ago, yeah, I'd have insisted on something ridiculously over the top, but that's not me anymore."

I acknowledged her words with a thoughtful nod. My friend had changed a lot since we first met, having rediscovered her true self. I was determined to help her in any way I could. "Okay. What's the plan? What can I do?"

"Well, we've decided on a small ceremony at city hall and then back to our house for a big party. We're going to rent one of those big tents for the backyard, with heaters, of course, as it will be October. Oh, and a small dance floor."

"Really? At your house?"

"Yeah, I mean, I've sung at so many weddings that they've kind of all blurred into the same night, and I don't want that to happen to mine. I want something small and intimate with close friends and family." She leaned back and stared at me intensely while Gunner placed his head on her lap. "Vic, I want you to know that if we were having a church wedding, I'd ask you to be my maid of honor."

Despite our close friendship, my mouth fell open. "Me?"

"Well, duh." She rolled her eyes. "You know you're my best friend."

A lump formed in my throat, and tears pricked my eyes. Growing up, I had no close friends and dreamed of moments like this. "And if you were having a church wedding, I'd say yes."

"Good. So that's settled, then. Now, are there any extra cookies? I'm going to allow myself one, and then I'll start watching my weight for the wedding."

"There's a few extras. Hold on." I handed her a plate with two cookies.

Stephanie held one up, inspecting it. "Baby theme cookies. Are you trying to tell us something?"

"Not me. That's for sure. Typically, you have to have sex to get pregnant, and unless I gestate babies like an elephant, then no. Not me."

We both laughed, but something deep inside tugged at me. I ignored it, not wanting to face whatever it was. "They're for Darcy. You've met her. She runs the animal shelter. Anyway, yesterday she revealed to us she's expecting."

"How do you find the time to volunteer there, work, and make cookies? Just knowing how busy you are exhausts me."

"Oh right, says the woman who works, teaches private music lessons, and plays in a band."

"Touche. I guess it keeps us out of trouble." She examined the cookie again. "This is almost too cute to eat, but not quite." She took a bite. "I've said it before, and I'll say it again: You need to sell—" She froze.

"What's wrong? Are they horrible? Did you chip a tooth?"

"No. I've just had the most amazing idea ever."

"Uh-oh."

Stephanie took a deep breath. "Will you please, please, please make my wedding cake?"

# 4

"ARE YOU CRAZY?"

"A little, but that's beside the point. Come on, Vic. It's a great idea."

"I make cookies, not cakes," I insisted. In fact, it was narrower than that. I made cookies I could decorate. Sugar cookies, gingerbread cookies, and occasionally a gingerbread house. That was it. I couldn't make a cake worthy of a wedding. Especially Stephanie's wedding. Surely, she knew that.

But Stephanie shook her head. "Not true. You made that one last New Year's Eve for Abby. It was black and had fireworks all over it."

"Well, yeah." She wasn't wrong, except for one technicality. "I decorated it, but the cakes were from mixes. I can't make you a wedding cake from a mix."

"Mix schmix." She dismissed my concerns with a wave of her hand. "It was delicious and, more importantly, something personal and unique. You made it special by designing it with Abby in mind, and I would love to have something personal like that for my wedding."

I pretended to write notes. "Gotch ya. One black firework cake."

"Ha, ha, you know what I mean."

I tilted my head back and released a defeated sigh, causing Gunner to glance in my direction. "What if I screw it up?"

"You won't."

"You're not going to take no for an answer, are you?"

"Nope." Stephanie stood and stretched, much to Gunner's dismay. "I know it's a big ask—okay, a huge ask—but I know you'll do an amazing job and make something special."

I stood, too. Stephanie was my best friend. Even though we'd only known each other for a little over a year, we'd grown close fast. I supported her through an emotional time, and she'd been a shoulder to cry on when the absence of Daniel hit me like a ton of bricks, holding me tight while I sobbed until there were no more tears left. Growing up, kids avoided me; likely, their parents didn't want them to befriend the child of an addict, so Stephanie was my first real friend. There wasn't much I wouldn't do for her. "How can I say no to that?"

"Yay," she said, hugging me. "Now I gotta run and tell Jenna, then get home. Busy days ahead. We'll talk tomorrow."

Stephanie left like a glamorous hurricane, and I plopped down beside Gunner. He sat up and licked my cheek. "I don't know about this, Gungun. What have I gotten myself into?"

# 5

The rain ran down the stairs and into the metro as I made my way up to the sidewalk. At the top, a crack of thunder startled me to the point where I nearly dropped my groceries. I was completely unprepared for the rain. It had been unseasonably warm when I left my apartment for the grocery store, but since then, the storm had rolled in and, with it, a shift in temperature.

My only hope was that the storm would pass as quickly as it arrived because waiting it out wasn't an option. My windows were open, and Gunner would be terrified. Not only that, my bags were filled with baking supplies for Stephanie's trial cakes as I intended to test a few recipes. If the bags of flour and sugar got wet, they'd be ruined, and this trip would have been for nothing. But I had no choice. I had to get home to Gunner.

The dark clouds reflected my mood as water ran down my face and through my clothes. My sneakers splashed through puddles, soaking my socks and the groceries hanging from each hand. I would be lucky to salvage anything.

As I stepped into the building's foyer, I tried to shake most of the rain onto the doormat before entering my apartment. "Gunner, I'm back," I called out.

He didn't come running to greet me. Poor thing. He was likely hiding in the bathroom. I placed the groceries on the counter and went to find him. "Gungun?" He didn't come. I checked the bathroom, but he wasn't there. Nor was he under the futon or in the closet. My stomach knotted. There wasn't anywhere else to hide. Oh God. The window. I turned and saw that the screen was gone.

And so was Gunner.

I leaned out the window as far as I could. The screen lay in the bushes below. "Gunner? Gunner!"

A fierce flash of lightning and the deafening boom of thunder ripped apart the sky. My poor boy would be terrified. Fear surged through me like a tsunami. What if he ran onto the street and got hit by a car? What if his panic drove him so far away that he couldn't find his way home?

Forcing my wet shoes back on, I raced outside. I checked under the porch stairs, the backyard, and Matt's car. Where had he gone? Running up and down the street, I shouted his name while the rain ran down my face almost as fast as my tears.

After twenty minutes of searching, I collapsed on the front steps as the rain let up and remained there until I heard the phone ringing through the still-open window. I was set to ignore it. Then I remembered Gunner's tag. Maybe someone found him. I jumped up and raced for the phone. "Hello?"

"Yeah, hi. I think I have your dog."

"Gunner? You have Gunner? Is he okay? Please tell me he's okay. He's terrified of thunder and must have pushed out the screen at the window. I've been searching for him since I came home. How is he? Is he scared? Is he hurt?"

"He's fine," a man said, his voice calm. "Safe and sound."

A wave of relief crashed over me, overwhelming every cell in my body until I thought I might collapse. My heart raced as I took in the news that he was safe, and yet, so rattled with emotion, I missed the caller giving me his address and had to ask him to repeat it. "But that's right next door."

"Oh, yeah? Well, nice to meet you, neighbor," said the caller. "Want me to bring him by?"

"No. It's okay. I'll come get him." Seconds later, I stood knocking on his door.

It opened immediately. "Wow. I think you were knocking before I'd even hung up the phone," the man said.

"Yeah," I said, barely seeing him as I looked beyond him, searching for Gunner. From where I stood, I could see down the hall and into the living room. And there was Gunner's tail, poking out from under a coffee table. "Gunner?" His tail thumped on the floor.

He was safe. He was okay.

At that moment, everything caught up with me. Fear. Anguish. Panic. Relief. I burst into tears. Standing in this stranger's foyer, it was all I could do to stop my sobs. It took me an embarrassingly long time to regain my composure, and I nearly began again when a little boy appeared holding out a box of tissues. I pulled three from the box and blew my nose.

"Sorry," I said, my voice shaky. "But Gunner means everything to me. I couldn't handle losing him. Not when he was scared, not if he thought I abandoned him. His original owner left him to die in an empty apartment. That's why he was at the animal shelter. It took a while for him to trust me. I rarely leave him alone and would hate to think that he thought I left—"

The warmth of the man's hand on my shoulder stopped me mid-sentence.

"It's okay. He's fine," my neighbor said soothingly.

"I know. You're right." I took a deep breath and turned my face to his, finally calm enough to take in my surroundings, beginning with the person who had rescued Gunner. My neighbor was a couple inches taller than me, with short blond hair and bright cerulean eyes that crinkled in the corners when he gave me a big, friendly grin. His demeanor radiated kindness, like the warmth of a summer sunrise, and I began to relax.

"Come on in. He's under the coffee table. We can't seem to coax him out, which is why it took so long to call you. I couldn't get to his tag, and I didn't want to scare him. He's been here since the storm started. He ran right past us and into the house when I opened the door."

All I could think about was wrapping Gunner in my arms, but knowing he was nearby and was okay prevented me from barging into this stranger's house. "I can't. I'm soaking wet. I don't want to drip on your floor."

"Don't worry. That's what mops are for." He led me into the living room, and I dropped onto my knees by the coffee table. Gunner's big eyes peered into mine as I reached out and gently stroked him behind the ears. "You had me worried, big guy. How about we go home now?" Gunner extended a paw and placed it on my arm but didn't budge.

"He's okay for a minute. Why don't I get you a towel and something warm to drink? You're shivering."

"I am?" I hadn't noticed. "Huh. Well, thanks, but I should really get him home." The words had barely left my mouth when a crack of thunder shook the house.

"Looks like round two," the man said. "I don't think he's going to leave there anytime soon."

I sighed. "Maybe you're right."

"I'm Alex, by the way, and my son's name is Noah."

"Nice to meet you both," I said. "I'm Vicki, and, well, you've met Gunner." Glancing down at Gunner, I spotted the small puddle I'd left on the floor. "If you pass me a cloth, I'll wipe the floor. It's a bit wet."

"No problem. Be right back."

Alex returned with a large bath towel he held out to me and then mopped the floor.

"I can do that," I insisted.

"Oh, no worries. All done. Now sit, and I'll get you something warm to drink."

Since I was still shivering, I agreed.

"Tea? Coffee? Something stronger?"

"Tea would be perfect."

"Be right back then."

I smiled at Noah, who sat on the floor close to Gunner, then assessed the living room for somewhere to sit that wouldn't be ruined by my wet clothes. Alex had a leather sofa, so I laid the towel down and sat there. Across from me was a matching leather armchair with a stack of books beside it on an end table. The coffee table and end tables were all pine. He'd painted the walls of the living room sage green and, combined with the wood and the camel color of the sofa and chair, created a harmonious, earthy palette.

It was easy to imagine Alex reading to Noah in the armchair. "You're a lucky kid," I said to Noah, who turned to me, no doubt wondering what I was talking about. "And thank you for rescuing Gunner. I'm so grateful you found him." The boy gave me a smile similar to his father's.

Alex returned, placing a tray of tea on the coffee table. "My mother's from England," he said. "She always has this tray ready for when she's over."

"I like her already," I said.

"Milk, sugar, or lemon?" he asked, then picked up a cup. "So, how long have you been living next door?"

"Two years. I moved here from Ottawa."

"Oh, nice. My parents used to take my brother and me skating on the canal once a year. I bet you did that all the time."

"No, never." Alex's eyes went wide with shock, but admitting to him we were too poor to afford skates when I was a child or that, later on, skating wasn't a Kent-approved activity wasn't going to happen. "I can't skate, although my friend Jenna has tried to help me. She used to be a competitive figure skater. Now, she's teaching her daughter Abby to skate. You should meet them. I don't know how old your son is, but they must be close in age. Abby's just started kindergarten." I took a sip of tea, which was too hot. So be it. Anything to stop talking.

If my rambling annoyed him, he didn't show it. "Noah will start kindergarten next year, so they are pretty close in age. It would be great if he had a playmate close by. That makes things a lot easier," Alex said.

"I bet. And Abby's super friendly and outgoing, so I'm sure they'd have fun together."

"I take it your house is divided into apartments?"

"Yeah. I live on the main floor in the smallest apartment. Jenna and Abby live upstairs. They used to live directly above me, but recently, they moved in with Matt, who lived across the hall from Jenna. His apartment is huge and spans two floors, which is why mine is so small. Josh and Sylvanna moved into Jenna's old apartment. Josh is Abby's biological father, and he wanted to be close to her, and I'm going to stop talking now because it sounds like a soap opera, but it's actually pretty great for everyone."

Alex leaned forward. "No, don't stop. I feel like I have the inside scoop on the street."

"Please don't think I'm a gossip. These people are my close friends." I began chewing the inside of my cheek. The warmth radiating from his eyes and smile sparked an unusual sense of trust within me, especially odd considering we had only just met. Yet, it was there, undeniable and compelling, leading me to open up. "I talk too much when I'm nervous or uncomfortable, and I'm uncomfortable right now because I intruded on your afternoon and got your floor all wet."

"Oh, God. I hope I did nothing to make you feel that way or imply that you were a gossip. It's kind of nice to learn about the neighborhood. I haven't had a chance yet, what with work and Noah," he said apologetically. "And honestly, you're not an intrusion. Rescuing Gunner is going to be a story Noah tells for a while. Right, buddy?"

Noah glanced at his dad from where he sat on the floor beside Gunner and nodded.

After that, silence filled the room—not exactly awkward, but not the comfortable silence that exists between friends. Luckily, a kitchen timer sounded, prompting Alex to stand. "Be right back."

There was some distant clatter. Then, he promptly returned with a plate of muffins. "They need to cool for a bit," he said, placing them on the coffee table beside the tea tray.

"Wow. They smell amazing." As if on cue, my stomach growled.

"Noah, yours is on the kitchen table when you're ready."

"Yummy," Noah said and ran off.

"Here." He slid the plate to me, then, leaning in, lowered his voice to a conspiratorial whisper. "They're zucchini chocolate chip. But don't tell Noah. This is the only way I can sneak vegetables into him."

"My lips are sealed," I replied with playful seriousness, pretending to zip my lips together, locking them with an imaginary key, and tossing it over my shoulder. "So you made these yourself?"

His eyebrows arched in mock offense. "Don't sound so surprised."

"Sorry, was it that obvious?"

"Yeah, it was," he replied, his laughter ringing clear and genuine, brightening the room like a ray of sunshine through the storm clouds.

I laughed along with him before picking up a muffin and taking a bite. Wow. They were really good. "These are delicious."

"Thanks. It's my own recipe. I had to play around for a long time for Noah to be fooled. I likely won't win a parenting award, but what can you do?"

"Well, if they don't give you a parenting award, you should definitely win a cooking one."

He grinned. "Thank you. And you are welcome to try my food anytime."

"If everything is this good, I will hold you to that," I said, finishing my muffin and brushing a few crumbs from my lips onto a napkin as I glanced out the window. "Looks like the rain has stopped, and I don't hear any more thunder." My gaze lingered on the clearing skies a moment longer before returning to Alex. I'd enjoyed talking with him, and time had flown by, but the cozy room, filled with the aroma of muffins and remnants of our shared laughter, suddenly felt too intimate for near strangers. "Gunner and I better let you get back to your evening. I imagine Noah needs dinner, and your wife will be home soon."

"Yes, and no. It's just me and Noah."

The heat of embarrassment flushed through my cheeks. While I probably wasn't the first to make that mistake, what if he thought I was fishing for information? To prevent any more embarrassment, I forced myself to look him in the eye. "Oh. Sorry. I just assumed, because of, well, Noah I guess. It's just Gunner and me, too. Where is he, anyway? I didn't notice him leave his spot under the coffee table. At least I know he's here somewhere. Gunner?" Thank goodness for Gunner. He was a welcome conversation changer.

Noah's laughter echoed from within the kitchen as we moved toward the hall. Seconds later, Gunner sauntered out, his movements leisurely and content, obviously chewing on something.

"Looks like Noah might have shared his muffin. I hope that's okay," Alex said. "I know dogs can't have chocolate, but there's not a lot in them, and usually, Noah picks out all the chocolate chips to eat first."

"I'm sure it's fine. Typically, he has a gut of steel." As I hooked up his leash, I planted a kiss on his head. "All right, big guy. Let's get home."

Stepping out into the night, the cold air hit with the crispness only a post-storm evening could muster. The storm's earlier fury was now replaced with serene darkness, and the earlier chaos seemed like a distant memory. The thought of cozying up at home with Gunner was suddenly all that mattered. There would be no cake baking tonight, but that was okay.

"Well, I hope we see you around," Alex called out. "I'd love to get together and hear more about the neighborhood."

"Anytime," I agreed, somewhat surprised by my eagerness to see Alex again. But I told myself not to overthink it. I enjoyed our interaction, and it didn't hurt to know your neighbors. So, with that in mind, I let the possibility of a new friendship light the way home, a small but significant comfort against the backdrop of a stressful and chaotic day.

# 6

"SMELLS AMAZING HERE, AS usual," Stephanie announced as she entered my apartment, making me startle from her unexpected arrival. With all my attention focused on icing cookies, I didn't hear her enter the building. "Are you practicing for my cake? If so, I'd love to taste a sample."

"Not quite yet. These are cookies for my next-door neighbor," I said, smiling. I loved that Steph was the drop-by-unannounced type, even if it made my heart race when she caught me by surprise.

Stephanie raised an eyebrow. "Your neighbor? Do tell." She pulled out a chair and sat down.

I continued to ice the cookies while replying. "I didn't tell you this, but Gunner got out during that storm several days ago. I freaked out and searched everywhere, but it turned out he was right next door. Alex, my neighbor, called to let me know. These cookies are a thank you."

"Interesting. And this Alex, is he male, and if yes, is he single?" Stephanie asked in her typical direct manner.

"What?"

"Your neighbor. Is he single?" Stephanie pronounced each word slowly.

Setting down my piping bag, I faced her. "I understood, and yes, he's single. Divorced. He also has a kid. A son. Noah. I meant, why are you asking?"

"Because you're baking cookies for him."

"I bake cookies for everyone. You know that." Even though that was true, it kind of felt like a lie. These cookies seem to carry an extra layer of significance. Maybe because our introduction was caused by such a stress-inducing event? Surely, it had little to do with how much I'd enjoyed our conversation.

"I know," she conceded, drumming her fingers on the table. "Still. How old is he? Is he cute?"

"I don't know, but he must be close to our age, and yes, he's cute." I returned to piping so she wouldn't catch my expression over the memory of his kind smile.

"And how old is his kid?"

"Young, but not a baby. He's a bit younger than Abby."

Her eyes lit up. "So, what are you waiting for? Go drop those cookies off and ask him out."

"Um, no. But I will drop off the cookies."

"Vic, you have to move on past Daniel. It's been over a year—nearly two," Stephanie reminded me gently as if I didn't remember. "You told me going your separate ways was the right move, and you have no regrets. So what's holding you back from meeting someone new?"

"Where should I begin? Fear, insecurity, doubt, to name a few. I also think..." My voice trailed off, not wanting to admit my secret hope, foolish as it might be. "Never mind."

"No. Finish that sentence. Please."

I looked down at the food coloring staining my hands. "I think part of me is hoping that one day Daniel will show up at my door again."

Stephanie stood and drew me into a hug. "Oh, my dear sweet friend."

"It's okay. I know in my heart that it's silly," I rushed to assure her as much as myself. "What we had was beautiful, but I know that chapter of my life is done. And honestly, I love my life. Great friends, Gunner, a job I love. I don't need anything—or anyone–else."

"Well, you do have great friends," Stephanie joked, but her skeptical expression told me I hadn't convinced her. Honestly, I had to wonder myself. I'd been insisting my life was complete with increasing frequency. Was I trying to convince myself?

I pushed Stephanie's comments out of my mind as I approached Alex's front door and knocked.

A few seconds later, Alex opened the door, smiling when he recognized me. "Hi, Vicki."

"Hi," I replied, suddenly feeling awkward. I held out the plate of cookies. "This is for you and Noah. I wanted to thank you again for the other day."

"I really didn't do much, but thank you." He took the plate. "Do you want to come in for a moment? Noah's just putting his pajamas on, so I'll need to put him to bed soon, but I have some time." Alex stepped back, gesturing me inside.

"Um, okay. Thanks," I agreed, surprising myself. But Alex's voice, so deep and smooth, swirled around me, drawing me into his house like one of those old-timey canes from a black-and-white movie.

"No Gunner today?" he asked.

"No, he's had a busy day, so he's already sleeping. He barely raised an eyebrow when I left." I stepped into his foyer and looked around. "You know, I was too shaken up the other day to notice, but I think your house is nearly identical to mine, but the mirror image and you probably don't have the bonus area Matt has above the alley. But other than that, I think this is what my house would have looked like before it was divided into apartments. Actually, I think your living room is my entire flat."

"Really? That's small," Alex said, then his eyes went wide with embarrassment and concern. He chuckled nervously. "Oops, sorry. There's nothing wrong with small. I hope I didn't offend you."

"No. No offense taken. It really is small, but it suits me. And it will only take me five seconds to give you the grand tour." Oh my gosh. Did I kind of invite him over?

"I look forward to it," Alex replied, his smile returning. "Let's go into the kitchen. I'm curious to see what's under the foil."

I followed him into the kitchen, and wow, what a kitchen. The far wall was flanked with bi-folding patio doors, which opened to the backyard. This was combined with the choice of white for the walls and cupboards. Far from being stark, I saw them as a canvas upon which the day's varying lights would play and vary. Butcher block countertops and the seamless extension of the wooden floors into what was clearly the heart of this home warmed the space and added a tangible connection to the rest of the house. With state-of-the-art appliances, functionality was balanced effortlessly with aesthetics. The layout centered on a U-shaped configuration, one side of which was a peninsula with stools where I imagined Alex and Noah sharing many moments and conversations. Things I never experienced as a child.

"I think I'm in love," I said, running my hand across the butcherblock. "I remember seeing contractors coming and going. And now I know why. This is stunning."

"Thanks," he said, placing the plate on the counter. "I might have gone a bit overboard, but I got a good deal on the house, so I thought, why not?"

"I don't remember seeing a for sale sign."

"That's because there wasn't. I bought it from my uncle. Or at least the bank and I did." He peeled back the foil from the cookie plate. "Oh my god, look at these. Did you make them?"

Feeling a blush creep into my cheeks, I nodded. "I did."

Alex selected a cookie and took a bite. The corners of his eyes crinkled with delight as he chewed. "Well, these are amazing," he said, his voice slightly muffled by the mouthful of cookie. "And they taste as good as they look."

"Thank you. You set the bar high with your muffins."

His infectious laughter filled the kitchen. "Honestly, these are so good. I'd love to sell these at the bakery."

"You work at a bakery?"

"Yeah, at Dolci Momenti."

"I've been there before. And Matt's there all the time."

"Good to know. Next time I bring some baked goods home, I'll drop some off." He held up another cookie, examining it closely. "I'm a pastry chef, but I don't have this kind of artistic talent. I can work with fondant and gum paste to create flowers and bows, but when people ask for character cakes, that's a whole other set of skills. What bakery do you work at?"

"Oh no. I'm no pastry chef. I work at an art store."

"Really? Well, you must also be an artist based on the icing design."

"Thanks. I don't know if I'd call myself an artist, but I do enjoy—"

Noah interrupted our conversation, calling out from upstairs. "Dad, I can't find Mr. Puffin."

"He's down here, in the living room," Alex replied. The sound of soft footsteps paddled down the stairs, and moments later, Noah walked into the kitchen with a stuffed puffin under one arm and wrapped the other around Alex's leg.

"Hi, Noah," I said, bending slightly to meet his gaze.

"Hello," replied Noah, and Alex placed a loving hand on his head.

"So where was I?" Alex said. "Oh yes, your talent."

"I think we covered that," I said in an effort to shift the focus away from myself. "Why don't you tell me how long you've been at the cafe?"

"Quite a few years now. I started there right out of culinary school. And that's it. Been there ever since. Great people, decent pay, regular hours–early hours–but still. And I'm lucky. My mother comes over every morning at four to take care of Noah until daycare opens."

"Four? Oh, wow."

"Yeah, I couldn't do it without her, but I'm not sure how much longer it's sustainable. She's hardly an old lady, but it's a grueling schedule. Because of that, I've been trying to start a wedding cake business on the side to see how that goes, but it's a challenge with Noah. My ex-wife has Noah once a month, so I experiment a lot in the kitchen then. And if a friend gets married, I offer to make their cake for free."

"You do wedding cakes?"

"Yeah, or other celebration cakes. Birthdays, graduations, that kind of stuff."

"Interesting." I tried to restrain the excitement in my voice. This seemed too serendipitous. Should I ask him for help, or would that be overstepping our newfound friendship? Maybe I'd tell Stephanie about him, and she could hire him. Yes, that's what I'd do. Or would she be disappointed in me?

Noah's yawn interrupted my train of thought and signaled that it was his bedtime and time for me to leave.

"Well, I better go." I squatted down to talk to Noah. "I baked some cookies for you and your dad to thank you for helping Gunner. I know it's late, so you can have one tomorrow."

Noah nodded, hugging his dad's leg tighter.

"I better put this guy to bed."

"Right. Well, enjoy the cookies. It was nice talking to you again."

"Next time, you can tell me about the art store."

"Fair enough." Huh. Next time. I kind of liked the sound of that.

# 7

GUNNER AND I WERE out for a run, but instead of running our entire route, we detoured and stopped at the top of Mount Royal. "Break time," I said to him.

He gave me a quizzical look, with reason, as it had been several months since we'd stopped there. Still, he remembered exactly where to go and sniffed the ground before circling and sitting down with a contented sigh. Despite the cold, I removed my backpack and sat beside Gunner, leaning against a tree next to 'our spot.' 'Our spot' was a rock where Daniel had carved our initials with a drill. V + D. He'd done that right before he left for Hong Kong, immortalizing our brief courtship in stone.

This place wasn't my only reminder of Daniel. A tattoo on my hip and one on my wrist reminded me daily of all that we shared. And then there was the picture I kept under my pillow. Having it there provided comfort, like a two-dimensional teddy bear. And occasionally, I'd reveal my deepest feelings and thoughts to it, like those worry dolls I'd seen for sale in a gift shop downtown. In that sense, it was cathartic, but conversely, one might argue that constantly reminding myself of him when we were no longer together was a form of self-torture.

But Daniel had shown me what it meant to be loved, and I liked the person I became because of that. Stronger. Confident. Comfortable with myself. And sometimes, I needed those reminders because my past never faded too far into the background. My mother's neglect and Kent's control hovered close, eliciting feelings of inadequacy and self-loathing. But thoughts of Daniel helped me block them out.

But enough reflection. That's not why I ran to the lookout. My decision to stop there was based on my need to find inspiration for Stephanie's cake. As the spot was beautiful and close to my heart, I thought it would stimulate my creativity, especially in the area of love.

Opening my backpack, I pulled out water for Gunner and a pad and paper for myself and began. Before I knew it, I was sketching a simple maple leaf, then another. Soon, I'd sketched a cascade of them on a three-tier wedding cake. Then I kept going, but instead of another cake, I designed a cake topper. Instead of a stiff image of a bride and groom, I drew Stephanie, emphasizing her beauty and gracefulness. The way she carried herself with joy and confidence. Her eyes were bright with hope for the future, and her smile spoke volumes of love. I sketched Jake behind her; his arm wrapped protectively around her waist as if there was nowhere else he'd rather be.

I stopped as a tear hit the page. Daniel had held me like that. Dammit. It's not like I thought Daniel and I would get married. From the night of our first kiss, I knew our time together was limited to six weeks. And I have no regrets. So why was I crying now?

A chill ran through my body, so I packed up and kissed my hand before placing it on our carved initials. "Time to go," I whispered to Gunner, my jaw aching with unshed emotion. He jumped up, unaware I was leaving another piece of my heart behind. How long until there was none left?

We set off down the path, and despite the bright sun, the trail felt cold and dark. The blazing reds and yellows of early fall had faded, leaving behind dried, brown leaves clinging to branches in defiance of the changing season. Maybe I wasn't alone in my failure to let go.

Both sweaty and chilled from our run, I decided a hot bath would warm me up and soothe my soul. I ran a tubful of hot water and poured some vanilla bubble bath into it. The tendrils of steam reached for the ceiling, curling around each other like a pair of lovers. I laughed at myself for imagining that image—I definitely had love on the brain.

As I was about to step in, the phone rang. *Daniel? Was he thinking of me right now, too?*

I rushed to answer. "Hello?"

"Hi. Vicki?" Not Daniel. Of course, not Daniel. This silly behavior of mine had to stop.

"Yes, it's me."

"Oh, good. You sound younger on the phone. Anyway, it's Alex from next door. I'm so sorry to bother you, but your number was in my cell phone from the storm incident, and I desperately need help. I have two pies that need baking, and as I placed them in the oven, I realized the oven didn't heat. I've checked everything, but I can't figure it out. Luckily, it's still under warranty, but that doesn't help me tonight. Normally, I'd go over to my parents' place, but they're getting their kitchen remodeled, and I can't go to the bakery because this is for my side business. So, I hate to ask you this, but can I please use your oven?"

"Right now?" All I could think of was my lovely, warm bath.

"Oh. It's a bad time. I'm sorry. I'll figure out something else."

"No. It's fine." I could have one later.

"Are you sure?"

"Yes. Of course."

"Thank you. You're a lifesaver."

"Gunner, we're going to have company," I said, hanging up the phone. His tail thumped on the floor.

I'd barely managed to drain the tub and throw on some sweats when Alex knocked at the door. I opened it to find him and Noah, both with their arms full. Alex with his two pies and Noah with an armload of books.

"Come on in, gentlemen," I told them. "I've already turned the oven to three-fifty to get it going. I figured you could adjust it if that wasn't the temperature, but at least it's on the way."

"That's perfect. Thanks again," he said, walking past me and into my living room. "I've got to drop these off tomorrow, and I'd feel awful if I didn't deliver on one of my first orders."

"Well, I hope they fit. My oven is small, like the rest of my place."

He placed the pies on the counter and adjusted the temperature. "Your place is cute," he said. "I love the colorful end table and chairs. It has a lot of personality."

"You're being generous, but thanks."

The oven beeped, prompting Alex to place the pies in the oven. He then pulled a timer out of his coat pocket and set it. "Once again, you're a lifesaver."

"So, pies?" I asked. "I thought you made cakes."

"Well, how about we say desserts to keep it simple, but the truth is, cakes are my specialty."

"What flavor are you cooking?"

"Cranberry-Almond Apple Pie."

"Sounds fancy."

"Let's hope the customer thinks so."

"Daddy, story," said Noah through a yawn. He'd climbed onto the futon with Gunner at his feet.

"If you don't mind, I'll sit and read to Noah so we're out of the way while you do whatever you need to do."

"Thanks, but you can see by the size of my apartment that I don't have anywhere to go."

"You know what they say, size doesn't matter."

"Oh, really now? Is that right?" I teased.

"So I've heard. Not that I'd know personally." He laughed as he blushed and ran a hand through his hair. "I'm going to sit down and read to Noah now."

"Good idea," I said, grinning, as I began to assemble the ingredients for lunch the following day. While I made a sandwich for myself and prepared food for Gunner, I listened to Alex reading to Noah. His deep voice was animated and invoked a surprising sense of nostalgia, reminding me of a teacher I had in grade two who read us a chapter of a story every morning. I loved storytime. It gave me a chance to escape my miserable life. I remember closing my eyes, conjuring up the images in my head, and watching the story unfold. That was a memory I'd nearly forgotten.

Alex caught me watching them and smiled.

"Daddy, it's stinky." Noah plugged his nose.

Noah was right. I smelled it, too, and turned to Gunner. "Sorry. That was Gunner, but wow, that's bad, even for him." I opened the living room window. "You okay, Gungun?"

He wagged his tail, then walked over to the door, tapping it with one paw to go out. I checked the time. "Not yet, Gunner. Wait until bedtime." He looked up at me and tapped the door again. "Hmm. Maybe I better take him out. We won't be long."

I was hooking up his leash when I heard an angry, gurgling sound. Gunner quivered and shook as he backed into my legs, and a second later, he had diarrhea. On my feet. And the smell—oh God—the smell was overwhelming and clung to the back of my throat, making me gag as it soaked through my sneakers. I couldn't move, not wanting to track poo through the apartment, but Gunner tapped again on the door. What if there was more?

"Here," Alex said, jumping up and grabbing the roll of paper towels from the kitchen. "Let me help. I'll take him outside. You get out of your shoes, and I'll help you clean up when I return. Noah, you stay on the couch and don't move."

Not knowing what else to do, I agreed, exchanging Gunner's leash for the paper towels. Slipping out of my shoes and socks under the watchful eyes of Noah, I laid out the paper towels like stepping stones and reached the bathroom to wash my feet before returning to face the challenge of the floor. With some paper towels and a garbage bag, I set about cleaning the mess. Despite my best efforts, the smell lingered at the back of my throat, nearly causing me to gag again. "I don't blame you for holding your nose," I told Noah.

With the worst of the mess scraped off the floor and my shoes placed into a bag and tossed outside, I set about washing the floor as Alex and Gunner returned.

"Well, we walked all the way to the park, and he went one more time, but nothing was going to go into the poop bag. It was like a river." He unhooked Gunner's leash, and I gave my dog a scratch on the head as he wandered over to his bed and curled up. "Looks like you're pretty much done. Is there anything I can do?"

"It's fine. You've done so much already. And I'm so sorry."

He shrugged. "These things happen. I could tell you some stories about explosive diaper poops if it will make you feel any better."

I held up my hand. "I'll pass, but thanks."

"So, did he eat anything weird today?"

"Nothing unusual—wait. He did pick something up off the street, but he was too quick for me to see what it was." I walked over to his bed and gave him a kiss. "Oh, Gunner, I do appreciate you trying to get outside."

"Wasn't it the other day that you said he had a gut of steel?"

"I did. I guess that came back to bite me in the ass, didn't it?"

Alex gave me his warm smile. "Can I use your bathroom to wash my hands?"

"Yes. Of course. It's the second door on the left."

Alex returned right as the timer sounded. "Perfect timing," he said.

"You mean saved by the bell?"

He chuckled while pulling the pies out of the oven and placing them in the box he'd carried them over with. "Well, what a night. It will be one I won't forget for a while. And thanks again for your oven."

"Anytime," I replied. Despite the chaos, it had been enjoyable having them over.

Alex was reaching for the door when it opened.

"Knock knock," said Stephanie, entering. "Oh, hello," she said to Alex, her surprise evident. Then she turned to me. "Why does your apartment smell so weird?"

Alex and I began laughing. I caught his eye and laughed harder, to the point where I was doubled over, tears streaming down my face. Alex was in a similar state. Stephanie eyed us warily, not understanding what sparked this sudden hysteria outburst. Every time I caught Alex's eye, the wave of laughter would strike again. After what felt like an eternity, we slowly calmed down, still chuckling at our private joke. My cheeks hurt from smiling so hard—it felt like forever since I'd laughed like that.

# 8

"HAS IT BEEN BUSY today?" I asked Isabelle as Gunner and I entered the store. Celine, Isabelle's tiny terrier, sauntered over to us from her sunny spot in the front window and gave me a sniff. Then she and Gunner entered the office and settled by the radiator for a nap.

"Not really. But it's Tuesday, and a cold one at that." Isabelle shut the store laptop and slid it under the counter. "We got that delivery of brushes this morning. Why don't you start with that?"

"Sure thing." After hanging up my coat and stowing my lunch in the fridge, I took a moment to give each dog a scratch. Then, I set about my task, opening the box to restock the brushes, all the while hoping the day would pick up in busyness. Stocking inventory was a simple task, and I didn't mind it, but this kind of work left me with too much time inside my head, which caused me to overthink things and eventually doubt myself. It shouldn't—I was in a good place, but still. That's how my mind worked.

Using my utility knife, I carefully opened the first box. This one contained brush sets, which I hung on the middle of the rack. These were among our biggest sellers and perfect for beginners and those taking classes, so we always ensured they were easy to find. Once painters advanced their skill and developed their style—a style as unique and individual as a fingerprint—they became more discerning in their choice of brushes.

Take Filbert brushes, which were the next item to stock. These brushes could create both broad and fine strokes and were particularly effective for blending away hard edges and creating soft shapes like petals and clouds. Daniel had painted my life with a Filbert brush. Not literally, of course, although he wrote Leonard Cohen lyrics on me with a Sharpie once. Daniel softened the rough edges of my life, mitigating its harshness with every tender, love-filled stroke. And the result was beautiful, infusing my life with color. And like a talented artist, his impact lingered because even after he left, my life continued to blossom.

The surprising tap on my shoulder caused me to drop the brushes in my hand. Whirling around, I found Alex standing there. Alex?

"I didn't mean to scare you," he said, cheeks red from the cold. "I called out several times, but you were so lost in thought."

"Oh, right. Sorry. I guess I was."

"No need to be sorry. I'm the one who snuck up on you. Anyway, I was downtown running some errands and thought if you were free, I could take you to lunch, as thanks for your oven the other night."

Lunch with Alex? A small flutter of excitement washed over me. Then nerves. But neither mattered, thank goodness, because I couldn't leave for lunch. "Thanks, but I've only been here an hour. I'm closing today. Maybe another time?"

His hopeful expression fell slightly, but his voice remained optimistic. "Yeah, sure."

"Now, hold on a minute," Isabelle called out from across the store. The old wooden floor creaked as she made her way toward us. "It's not busy. Feel free to take a break."

"Oh, well..." I scrambled to think of a reason not to go, but my mind was as blank as a new canvas. Why was lunch with Alex making me nervous? We were neighbors. Friends. It wasn't a date or anything. Stephanie would tell me to go. Clearly, Isabelle thought it was a good idea. Should I? Oh God, had the silence stretched out too long? Say something, for Pete's sake. "Okay. That would be great."

His face relaxed into a wide grin, warm enough to heat the store.

"Fantastic," he said, turning his attention to the floor.

Gunner had planted himself on Alex's foot. His tail began wagging with such vigor that it sent several paint bottles tumbling off the lower shelf, frightening him and causing him to pee a little. He then scurried behind me. I drew my lips into my mouth, trying not to laugh.

Alex squatted down and gently scratched Gunner behind the ears. "Don't worry, buddy. You can come too." The kindness in his voice practically melted my heart.

Isabelle tossed a roll of paper towels at me. "Oh, Gunner," she sighed. "We do love you."

Smiling at her, I knew I was fortunate to have her as a boss. "Alright, just let me wash my hands, and then we can get going," I said.

"Great," Alex said. "Gunner and I will wait outside."

"Are you sure you want to do that? It's not that he'll pee again; he doesn't normally have so many accidents, at least not until recently."

"Is that your way of saying his GI problems are because of me?"

"No, no. That's not what I meant." My cheeks flushed with embarrassment.

"I know. I'm teasing. Come on, Gunner. Let's go. I'm starving."

I washed my hands, grabbed my coat, and stopped at the front counter across from Isabelle. "I'll be back soon. Want me to take Celine?"

"No. You know how she hates the wind. Thanks though. Oh, and I hope I didn't go too far, intervening, but since things didn't work out with Oliver..." her voice trailed off, and she held up a hand before I could protest. "Yes, yes. I know you said you weren't interested, but this is a whole other story, isn't it—a cute guy showing up and asking you to lunch out of the blue?"

"Were friends. That's all."

"Whatever you say, just promise me you'll have fun."

I rolled my eyes, gave her a mock salute, and then joined Alex and Gunner on the sidewalk.

"Here we go then," Alex said, passing me Gunner's leash. "I know a great place nearby for a fast lunch, or if you have a favorite place, we can go there."

"No, I trust you. You're a professional. So long as it's takeout."

"Of course. Now follow me. It's a small little place where a friend of mine used to work. It doesn't look like much, but the food is incredible, providing you like falafel."

"I love falafel. Lead the way."

We walked along Sainte Catherine's, the sidewalk emptier than usual because of the wind and cold weather. The stiff breeze penetrated my coat and cut through me like a chilled knife.

I must have shivered because Alex said, "Sorry you're so cold. It's not far, I promise, and we should be out of the wind soon."

We turned off onto a side street, and Alex was right. The strength of the wind had diminished. We turned again before stopping in front of a takeout restaurant. Small or not, it was bustling with people, the line winding out the door, all eager for something warm to fill them up.

"Wait here, then we can find a park bench or something."

Despite the long line, it moved quickly, and minutes later, Alex returned with two warm pita sandwiches in a bag.

"Let's go find a spot to sit, preferably out of the wind," he said.

We found an empty bench in a small parkette, but not entirely out of the wind. So reluctantly, I stuck my hand in my pocket and pulled out a Montreal Canadians hat that used to belong to Daniel.

"Nice hat," Alex said. "You like hockey?"

I shrugged. "I don't hate it, but I don't watch it either. This hat...was a gift."

"Let me guess. From an old boyfriend?"

My mouth fell open. "How'd you know?"

"I'm no detective, but you have a funky, artsy style. That hat doesn't really suit your aesthetic. And since you're not a hockey fan, it must mean something to you. Boyfriend is an easy guess."

"That obvious, huh?"

Alex broke eye contact with me, opening the bag and pulling out some napkins. "Is he still around?" Alex asked.

"No. Not for a long time," I admitted. "As far as I know, he's not even in the country. But it's all good." I straightened my posture. "I just like the hat. That's all," I lied.

Alex's expression hinted that he wanted to ask something else but was hesitating. I took the opportunity to change the subject because a jumble of emotions somersaulted in my stomach. I'd grown accustomed to some because they always surfaced when I thought of Daniel, but today, something extra bounced around in the mix. Something to do with Alex. It was both scary and exciting, but also something I wasn't ready to face yet. "So, are we going to eat these falafels or what? The aroma is making my stomach growl."

"Sure thing," he said, passing me a pita. He tapped his against mine. "Cheers." We both took a bite.

"So, how long have you been at the art store?" he asked, wiping tahini sauce off his chin.

"About a year and a half. Working there is a dream come true."

"Go on. Why?"

"All I'd done before that was waitress, and while I liked it, I didn't want to make a career out of it. I love fine arts and always dreamed of an art-related career. When I was younger, I wanted to become a famous artist, and I actually have—" I stopped, taking a large bite of pita so I'd be chewing for a long time. Why was I telling him about this?

He waited patiently for me to finish my bite. "You're not comfortable talking about yourself, are you?"

I shrugged. "Not really. Is it that obvious?"

He nodded thoughtfully and said, "Well, I enjoy learning about you, Vicki, my neighbor with a nervous dog and working oven. So please continue. You actually have what?"

I cleared my throat to ease the sudden tightness. "Three charcoal sketches in a martini bar in Outremont."

"That's awesome."

"Yeah," I nodded and took another bite. "It's one of the most positive things that's ever happened to me, and it kind of kicked off some changes in my life."

He held my gaze for a long time. "I'm curious about these changes, but I don't want to press my luck and scare you away."

I leaned into him, giving him a playful nudge. "You think you're pretty smart, don't you?"

He shrugged. "I do my best."

We fell into a brief silence, both of us eating.

"Tell you what," Alex said, breaking the silence. "Since you shared something personal with me, I'll let you ask me anything you want."

"Anything?" I let the word hang in the air.

"I'm not going to regret this, am I?"

"We'll see," I teased. "But for now, do you mind if we start walking back. I don't want to be late."

"No problem," he agreed, and we began the trek back to the store.

"Now, let me think. What, oh what, should I ask?" My face contorted in mock seriousness. Then it hit me. "Okay, I know this isn't exactly what you meant, but you did say anything, right?"

"I did."

"Okay, then. My question is, will you bake me a wedding cake?"

His eyebrows arched, his eyes widened, and his mouth fell open. I nearly laughed. Clearly, he wasn't expecting that question. "A wedding cake? Really? For who? When?"

"My friend Stephanie is getting married and asked me to do it. I agreed, but it's beyond my skill level, and I'm terrified of letting her down. Originally, I was going to give her your name and have her ask you to do it, but it seems very important to her that I decorate it. So maybe it's something we can work on together?"

"Yeah. For sure. Thanks for thinking of me. This is a great opportunity. I bet we can come up with something amazing." His words rushed out, and his enthusiasm was infectious. For the first time since Stephanie asked, I was excited to make her cake.

"Did you want to think about it?" I teased.

"I better." His response was quick and humorous. "As you can tell, I'm kind of on the fence."

As we arrived at the store, he leaned down to pet Gunner, then turned to face me. "Let's talk later. This is the best news." The warmth in his voice matched the softness of his lips as he leaned in and kissed me on the cheek—my turn to be surprised. "Thanks for coming to lunch with me. I had a great time."

"Me too," I said as he walked away. The heat from his kiss lingered on my skin. People rushed by, and the city street buzzed with noise, but as my fingertips gently touched my cheek, I felt like I stood at the center of the universe.

## 9

When I admitted to Stephanie that I'd recruited help with her cake, she was supportive. "I didn't put too much pressure on you, did I?" she asked. I admitted that I had been nervous, but with Alex's help, I was excited to get started.

After revealing the date to Alex, we started right away. To his credit, with the wedding only four weeks away, he didn't panic like I did. He simply insisted that we meet up in his kitchen that Saturday night.

I was to bring a folder full of ideas. He was providing the ingredients.

Alex opened his door with the warm smile I was becoming familiar with—a smile I found both comforting and disarming. I kicked off my shoes and followed him into the kitchen, where Noah sat, eating a snack.

"Hi, Noah," I said, feeling not exactly shy but more like an intruder on his time with his dad.

"Hello," he replied. "Did you bring Gunner?"

"Not tonight. I left him playing with Poppet, my friend's dog."

"Can I see him again soon?" he asked. "The next time you cook with Dad?"

"Of course. I'm sure Gunner would like that, too."

"Okay, kiddo," Alex said. "Did you want to color while we cook?"

"Okay," he said through a yawn.

Alex passed Noah a coloring book and crayons and turned to me. "So I thought we'd offer them three flavors. Oh, and did the bride and groom confirm the tasting tomorrow?"

"Yes. They will be here around seven."

"Perfect. We'll also show them your designs, which I'm also curious to see. You mentioned them briefly, but I'm dying to take a look."

"Remember, Stephanie emphasized something personal, just so you're prepared."

"Ooo." Alex rubbed his hands together. "I love it. The more unconventional, the better."

"And what about your cakes? If the flavors are as complex as your pies, we're in for a treat."

He leaned against the counter, relaxed and at home in his state-of-the-art kitchen. "We need the basics, chocolate and vanilla. But I want to enhance them. Make it a bit more seasonal. I was thinking about Madagascar vanilla with a hint of bourbon, and instead of simple chocolate, we do a hot chocolate flavor. Then, to go with the fall theme, something earthy, like pumpkin, but with pumpkin pie spices."

"Holy, all those sound good and are way more impressive than plain old vanilla." I hoped my designs would do his flavors justice.

"What can I say? I think about these things a lot. Probably a little too much, if I'm being honest. Here, I'll prove it to you," he said, and picked up a notebook as the phone rang. "Noah, I bet that's Mommy. Go get it."

Noah slid off his chair and ran to the phone in the living room.

"His mom calls every Saturday night or Sunday morning, depending on her schedule," Alex said.

"You don't share custody?" I asked, then kicked myself for being rude. What if I touched on a sore spot? "Sorry. None of my business."

"It's fine, and no, we don't share custody. It's a long story," he said, his expression now serious. "My ex is not abusive or an unfit mother or anything like that, in case you're wondering."

"I'm not. It's just uncommon, that's all." If I had learned anything recently, it was that all families were different.

"I'll explain it another time. When Noah's not in earshot."

"You don't have to."

He shrugged. "We're friends. That's what friends do, right?"

"Right," I agreed, even though I could still recall the heat from his lips on my cheek. But I liked the idea of keeping our relationship simple. Friends were good. Friends were uncomplicated.

His smile returned as he gave me a gentle hip check before passing me his notebook. "As I was saying before the phone rang, here is my recipe book. Feel free to flip through the pages of my obsession. I would love to turn it into a cookbook one day. But that's for the future. For tonight, I've stuck Post-its on the recipes we're using." Then, he walked over to the pantry and began collecting ingredients.

Instead of reading the recipes, I stared at the wall of food. "I'm like a kid in a candy store. You're better stocked than most grocery stores."

"I did say obsession, didn't I?" he asked jokingly. "I like my job, but my determination to start my own business is growing. I desire to do something different and be known for something exceptional." He paused his hand on a jar of sugar. "Maybe it has nothing to do with baking. Maybe I'm still that guy who was told by his friends that getting married young and having a kid was a mistake. And okay, our marriage didn't last, but I don't regret any of it. So why do I feel the need to prove myself?" He squeezed his eyes shut as if pushing the thoughts out of his head. "Sorry. I don't know where all that came from."

"I get it. Sometimes it's easier to talk to someone who doesn't know your past or your friends."

He gave me a lopsided grin. "Yeah, but haven't we already established that we're friends?"

"We have. Friends who need to bake three cakes," I said. The conversation flowed effortlessly as he began assembling the ingredients. Alex's casual talk of his years at culinary school and his dreams of running his own business drew me in and I shared more about my love of art.

When Noah returned, we had just finished measuring the ingredients for the vanilla cake. "Can I help?" he asked.

Alex turned to me and winked. "That'd be great," he said, pulling a small apron out of a drawer. "Sit at the island," he told Noah. He did as told, and Alex passed him two small mixing bowls and some ingredients in plastic containers. "You're going to make the filling. Mix the dry ingredients with some milk and stir. Then it goes in the fridge. Got it?"

Noah nodded.

"I anticipated this," Alex whispered. "It's pudding mix. He'll make it, eat some, then move on to something else."

"I'm impressed," I said.

"It's not my first rodeo."

There's the expression that too many cooks spoil the broth, but Alex and I gelled. We worked quickly and efficiently, and instead of making one cake at a time, we made the chocolate and vanilla simultaneously, with me making the vanilla one and Alex the chocolate. All my stress disappeared as I focused on my task and enjoyed the lighthearted conversation. My spirits rose with each passing minute. Maybe this was what I needed, something new to focus on. I still didn't want to sell my cookies, but helping decorate cakes could be a way to let my creativity flow in a new way. Perhaps if Stephanie's cake worked out, Alex would ask me for help in the future.

I turned to grab a cloth and bumped right into Alex. My body tingled, starting in my chest where we'd collided and spanning out to the tips of my fingers and toes. I dodged around him before my face betrayed my attraction, wiped my hands, and threw the cloth at him. I returned to the batter, unsure how to process what happened. Yes, I'd felt sexual attraction since Daniel left, but it had been a long while since I'd felt...excitement. Electricity.

I filled a glass with water, hoping to drown my feelings, but there was a loud crash before I took a sip. Noah stared at the floor.

"Oh no, what a mess." I searched for something to wipe it up with. "Your poor floors."

"Don't worry. It's all part of the process." Alex reached under the sink for some rags.

We all stared at the brown mess.

"It looks like Gunner's poop," said Noah, making us all laugh. I grabbed a cloth and helped them clean up the mess. We all worked together, and soon the mess was gone. It sounds silly to enjoy a moment such as that one, but taking part in such a simple domestic scene left me grateful for being welcomed into their home and lives. Happy to have met them both, I decided then and there that I would try not to overthink anything between Alex and me. I would see where things went. If we stayed friends, okay. If things blossomed into something else, well, then I would take it one day at a time.

By the time the third cake was baking, all the dishes were done, the kitchen was tidy, and Noah slept on the couch.

"And now," Alex said, his eyes bright. "It's time for the sketches." He slid the folder across the countertop. "Amaze me."

"That's a lot of pressure."

"I know you can handle it. Now show me."

The folder, slightly worn at the edges from frequent handling, contained the culmination of my brainstorming. "Alright, well, the first one is the most traditional," I explained, handing him the sketch, "Except that instead of having flowers cascading down the cake, I wanted to make the cake look like it was full of flowers as if it's bursting with them. Can you see from the design that we cut a bit out on one side so it looks like they're coming from inside?"

"Yeah, I get it. This is cool. They almost look like butterflies."

"Yes! Exactly." The fact that he understood my vision ignited a flicker of confidence. "Each flower, emerging from within, represents something new and beautiful, in the same way that a union of two people holds that same potential."

"I'm impressed already. You've clearly put in a lot of thought."

With my confidence continuing to grow, I passed him the second sketch. "This concept is based on their first date, which was a hike. I thought we'd ice the cakes to look like the rugged, white bark of birch trees, well, the trunks anyway, and then instead of flowers cascading down, we create leaves. While their first date was in the spring, I thought we should use fall colors to tie into the October wedding. But, unlike the first cake, where the flowers were emerging, I want the leaves to convey the feeling of movement. Think of walking through a forest as they fall or how they dance through the air when it's windy. See how I've drawn some falling above the cake. Maybe we can use wire."

"Or we could actually have them move." He put the sketch down and paced. "Using edible paper, what if we suspended some leaves by thin threads above the cake? They'll move in the breeze, and then, as the happy couple are about to cut the cake, we have leaves fall down from above. Think how amazing the pictures would be."

"Do you think that would work?"

"We'd make it work. Think about it: a cake that's not only seen and eaten but experienced, a cake that invites the guests into a moment. It's amazing."

"I'm glad you like it," I said, unable to stop the smile from spreading across my face.

"Like it? I love it," he said. "What's next?"

"Okay, so this last one is a bit more playful." With a deep breath, I withdrew the last sketch and handed it to him. Knowing that there were two that he liked made giving him the third much easier. If he didn't like this one, at least we had options.

I gave him a few seconds to take it all in, then began my explanation. "So, as you can see, it's a simple three-tier cake in white. Jake is standing on the middle tier holding a paintbrush, as he is a housepainter. I am hoping it looks like he has just finished painting 'Just Married' on the cake."

"It does, and I love how a can of spilled paint is running down the first tier and pooling into a heart-shaped puddle."

"Thanks."

"So then this is Stephanie, sitting on top. I take it she plays the guitar."

"Yes. She's a musician." Beside Stephanie, her guitar case sat open, spilling tiny hearts and musical notes down the back of the cake. She is perched to look down at Jake and blow him a kiss.

Alex's gaze was intense, taking in every detail of the sketch. The silence stretched out for what felt like an eternity. Did he hate it?

"I don't know what to say." His face broke into a wide smile. "Again, this is amazing. I don't know how they will choose."

Suddenly, he wrapped his arms around me, lifted me off the floor, and spun us in a circle. "This is better than I ever imagined. I can do flavor and general design, but you have the creative vision and talent I'm lacking. I'd love to work together on future projects. We make an amazing team," he said, placing me back on the ground.

"We are pretty good together, aren't we?" I agreed, still encircled by his arms—a place I found very pleasant indeed. The warmth of his chest and the strength of his arms wrapped me in a feeling that was hard to pinpoint. Was it comfort? Belonging? The sensation was elusive, difficult to fully grasp or define, as if it were taunting me just out of reach.

Yet before I could figure things out, the sound of the timer cut through the moment, pulling us back to the task at hand.

Alex swiftly located the oven mitts and carefully extracted the last cake from the oven. "Perfect," he announced with a satisfied nod.

"It smells amazing," I said, as my stomach released a timely growl. "See, I wasn't lying."

"You should have said you were hungry. Can I get you something to eat?"

"I'm okay, thanks. I really need to get going. Gunner requires a bedtime walk, and I still need to get ready for work tomorrow."

"Of course." He gave me an understanding nod and walked me to the door. Each step took me away from the shared bubble of only a few moments ago. Doubts popped into my mind. Maybe our connection was a figment of my imagination. And if it wasn't, was I prepared for what it could mean?

As we reached the door, Alex paused, turning to face me. "You know, I'll say it again. There's a lot of potential here." His finger moved back and forth between us.

"Yeah." I agreed, swallowing hard. "I think you're right."

# 10

WHILE I HAD FINISHED the sketches of the cake, I continued to work on them during my lunch break at work the following day. Adding color, trying to make the designs more appealing. Sure, there was more detail than was needed, but it was so much fun I couldn't help myself. Waiting all day to show Stephanie and Jake the cakes nearly killed me. Considering I'd been reluctant to make them, the change in attitude was remarkable, but with Alex's help and enthusiasm, I was going to create something amazing. Make that we were going to create something amazing. I had to agree with him. We made a good team.

"What are you working on?" Isabelle asked, peering over my shoulder. "Something to show Oliver?"

"No, I haven't seen him since he hit the big time. I guess he's forgotten about all of us little people," I joked. "I'm actually working on designing a wedding cake for my friend Stephanie. What do you think?" I spread the three sketches across the table.

"Mon Dieu." She picked up the sketch of the silver birch tree. "These almost make me want to get married one day. Are you baking them, too? If they're anything like your cookies, the bride and groom are in for a treat."

"I'm working with Alex, the guy who invited me to lunch the other day. He's a pastry chef, and cakes are his specialty."

"If his baking is as good as your decorating, I'm doubly impressed. And, by the way, I'm not opposed to being a guinea pig if you need to test some flavors."

"Noted." I laughed, knowing that Isabelle had quite the sweet tooth. "He said we make a good team and hinted at collaborating on future projects. He wants to start his own business and says I bring skills he's missing. I think it might be fun—not that I'm planning on quitting, but it may be a way to make some extra money."

Isabelle ran a hand through her spiky hair as a fleeting expression crossed her face. It was too quick to read, leaving me with a bad feeling in my stomach.

She took a deep breath. "I know you love this store. I do, too, or I wouldn't still be here, but let's face it, neither of us will become rich, or even comfortable financially, by working here our entire lives. There's not a lot of opportunity for growth. If you can make some extra money, go for it. Who knows where it will lead?"

The room seemed to still as her words hovered in the air like an ominous mist. "Are you trying to tell me something?"

She hesitated, staring at the shelves full of art supplies. "No. Yes. An offer has been made to purchase the store. I don't know what Mr. Henderson will decide, but it wouldn't surprise me if he sells. He has little to do with the store now, and none of his kids want to run it. I wouldn't be surprised if he takes the money. Why not?"

My heart dropped into my stomach. "Oh. That sucks."

"Well, let's not panic yet. He casually mentioned it yesterday at our monthly meeting. And honestly, I couldn't read him one way or the other."

"Still..."

"Yeah."

The rest of my shift passed in a fog. All I could think about was the possibility of the store being sold. Closing up that night, my tradition of thanking the store for a good day and wishing it goodnight brought me to tears, and as the door lock clicked into place, I wondered how many more times I would perform this one simple act.

This store was more than a job to me. It was the place where I belonged. I loved the creaky wooden floor, the smell of paint, the sound of the bell chiming whenever someone entered the store, and the way Isabelle always made me laugh, even on my worst days. The customers knew us and would stop by to chat or give Gunner and Celine a treat. Mr. Powlski, next door, would shovel our walkway in winter, and I baked birthday cookies for Emma, who ran the dry cleaners.

So much more than the store was at risk, and my fears snowballed. I tried to use logic. The store might not get sold, and even if it did, it might still run as an art store, and Isabelle and I would continue to work there.

But logic didn't help, and my fear refused to be silenced while questions about my future loomed over my heart.

What would I do without the store? And more so, who would I be?

I'd heard that change is as good as a rest, and I hoped the saying was true because my anxiety over the store was put on the back burner, replaced by stress over the wedding cake designs. Pacing back and forth in Alex's living room, I tried to downplay the night's importance. It was dessert—a cake, nothing more. But this cake was for Stephanie's wedding, and I didn't want to disappoint her. Nor did I want to look like a fool. What if she claimed to love the designs simply to spare my feelings?

Who was I kidding? That wasn't Stephanie's style at all. She was as straightforward as they came, a trait that offered a strange comfort in this moment of self-doubt.

"Um, can I get you some tea? Or a Valium?" Alex asked.

I shot him a look that had him raising his hands in surrender. "Joking. Joking. I don't have any Valium, anyway."

"What if they hate all the designs?" I asked, dropping onto the couch.

"Then we come up with new ones."

Damn, that sounded so reasonable. "How can you be so calm?"

"Because that's what this meeting is about. Finding out what the customers like and what they don't. It's not personal."

I opened my mouth to protest but then shut it. Alex was right. Logically, I knew that, but my self-confidence was still fairly new, and constantly challenged because of that.

He sat down beside me. "Is there more than cake on your mind? I have a feeling that something else is contributing to your anxiety."

The look on my face must have confirmed his suspicions.

"Want to talk about it?" he asked.

I did. But to Alex? Maybe Stephanie. I'd talked to Daniel already, although talking to a photograph never led to sound advice.

Before I could decide, the doorbell rang, and I jumped up, nearly sprinting to the door. Alex, close behind, placed an arm around my shoulders and gave me a comforting squeeze before opening the door.

"Hey, Steph. Hi, Jake," I said as Stephanie walked in and hugged me. "This is Alex. Steph, you met him briefly the other night."

"Oh, right," she said. "The laughing guy with the pie emergency."

"Guilty as charged," Alex said, laughing. "Luckily, I'm back up and running with a working oven." He turned to Jake. "Alex. Nice to meet you."

Jake shook his hand. "Jake. Thanks for doing this."

"Happy to."

"Great, now let's get down to business," Stephanie said.

"Come into the kitchen and have a seat at the peninsula. What do you want to start with? Designs or cake?" I asked.

"Cake," Jake said.

Stephanie elbowed him playfully in the ribs. "Of course, Mr. Bottomless Pit would say that."

"Cake is never a bad place to start," Alex said.

"I like this guy, Vic," Jake said, giving me a wink.

As Stephanie and Jake took a seat, Alex unveiled the cakes, removing a large lid to reveal the three choices beneath. Carefully, he cut two slices from each cake, arranging one piece of each on two rectangular plates. He then presented the plates to Steph and Jake. To complete the setup, I handed out forks and glasses of water.

"This slice," Alex began, pointing to an end piece of cake, "is Madagascar vanilla with whipped maple bourbon filling." He continued, pointing in sequence. "The second is hot chocolate with marshmallow filling, and the third is pumpkin pie with cinnamon cream cheese. Take your time."

While I knew the cakes were delicious, as Alex let me taste them before Stephanie and Jake arrived, I still wrung my hands nervously. As if sensing my tension, Alex caught my eye. "Relax," he mouthed.

"Wow, wow, and wow," Stephanie said, placing her glass of water on the table. "I didn't know plain old vanilla could taste so...so...I don't know how to describe it."

"Complex," Jake said.

"Exactly." Stephanie placed a hand on his leg. "It's warm and sweet and yummy."

Just like Alex. Where the heck had that come from? My cheeks burned even though it had been a mere thought. Luckily, no one noticed.

Jake and Stephanie tasted the remaining two flavors. "Any of these would work. I love them all. I don't know how to choose," said Stephanie.

"Yeah, it's like being asked to choose a favorite child. How can you do that?" Jake added.

"How about we look at the designs, then?" Alex suggested. "Maybe a flavor profile will suit a specific cake. And don't forget, you can have different flavors for each layer."

Stephanie clapped her hands.

"Good to know," Jake said, wiping his mouth on a napkin.

Alex gently nudged me, prompting me to display my designs on the counter. Jake and Stephanie leaned in, examining them in silence. Time seemed to slow, each second stretching out painfully, allowing my mind to fill with self-doubt. They hated them. This was a mistake. What was I thinking by agreeing to this? Finally, unable to wait any longer, I blurted out, "You hate them, don't you?"

Both Jake and Stephanie turned toward me. "Are you crazy?" Stephanie asked.

"They're so good, I'm speechless," Jake said.

The tension knotting my body eased, and Alex slung an arm around my shoulder, pulling me against him. Suddenly, his lips brushed against my ear, sending shivers through my entire body. "I told you not to worry," he whispered.

"I don't know how we'll choose," Jake said. "I wish we could get them all."

"Yeah, but I don't want to weigh ten pounds more on our honeymoon," Stephanie said, still leaning over the designs, then suddenly she sat up straight. "Oh, I thought of something." She swiveled in her seat to face Jake. "Your mom is throwing that big dinner party for us, right?"

Jake nodded, and Steph faced Alex and me. "It's a family engagement dinner at her favorite restaurant. His mom said that despite not having much time before the wedding, she still wants to have as many steps in the process as possible. What if we had the one with us on the cake for that and then the one with the leaves at the reception?" she turned back to Jake. "What do you think, sweetie?"

"I think that's a great idea," he said, kissing her cheek.

"We'd have to change the writing. Instead of 'Just Married,' the writing could read 'She said yes,' "I suggested.

Stephanie squealed. "I love it, I love it."

"Great," Alex said, "But why don't you take tonight to think about it and let us know your final decision tomorrow. Then we can discuss all the details."

"Yeah, okay. We'll give you a call," Jake said, standing and extending his hand to Stephanie. They walked to the door.

"I knew I made the right decision asking you," Stephanie said, hugging me. Then she whispered, "And I really like Alex, but we'll talk about that another time." And with one more quick squeeze, she released me and walked down the stairs, holding Jake's hand.

With a final wave, Alex shut the door. "Can you relax now?"

"Yes. No. I don't know. There's so much to think about." My growing attraction was one of them, but now was not the time to think about that. Instead, I entered the kitchen and turned on the tap to fill the sink.

"What are you doing?" Alex asked.

"Helping you clean up."

"I can put it all in the dishwasher."

"Oh, right. I'm not used to such luxury," I said, my voice teasing.

"I guess they don't make them small enough to fit in your apartment," he joked.

"Ouch," I said.

"Truth hurts, doesn't it?"

I laughed. "Okay, you got me. I don't have a comeback for that."

We placed the dishes in the dishwasher, and I lingered, not wanting to leave.

"Do you want a glass of wine? We can toast to a job well done," Alex suggested.

"Thanks, but I don't drink. How about tea?"

"Tea it is."

"If you want wine, go ahead. It doesn't bother me. And I'm not a recovering alcoholic, in case you're wondering. My mom has addiction issues, and I simply chose a long time ago to avoid addictive substances. In case it's hereditary or something like that."

"You don't need to justify your choice to me," he said gently, turning on the kettle.

"I can't help it. People are always so shocked when I say I don't drink."

"I'm sorry people make you feel that way," he said. "You said your mother had addiction issues. How is she now, if you don't mind me asking?"

"Honestly, I don't know." I picked at my cuticles. "It's been years since I've seen her. I left home after finishing high school and never looked back. But I sometimes wonder about her and hope she is okay."

"Do you think you'll ever reach out? Not that you have to. Sometimes, we have to let things go."

"I think about it, but I'm not ready. Maybe one day. Maybe not. I have a good life, and I'm not sure if I'll ever be strong enough to go back."

"Sounds like you have a good group of friends."

"I do."

He placed two tea bags into mugs and poured water in. "I bought chamomile just for you," he said, sliding one over to me.

"How did you know I liked chamomile?"

"You have about ten different boxes of it in your kitchen."

"Oh. You noticed that?"

"Kind of hard not to. And since we will be working together, the least I could do was offer you your favorite tea from time to time."

"That's really thoughtful."

"That's what friends are for, right?"

"Right."

"You know what friends are also for?"

"What's that?"

"Telling their woes to."

"Woes?"

"Yes, you know, troubles, trials, tribulations. Now, what's bothering you?"

"It's nothing."

He tilted his head and raised his eyebrows. "I don't believe you. Now come with me."

I followed him into the living room, and we sat together on the couch.

He leaned back and put his feet up on the coffee table. "Now tell me."

I sipped my tea, feeling his eyes on me. At the same time, the uncertainty from this morning's conversations with Isabelle came rushing back. "It's nothing. I mean, I'm fine. I talked to Daniel." Oh shit. Why did I say that? Why mention Daniel?

"Daniel?" He echoed, his voice laced with surprise.

*Way to go, Vicki. You finally find someone you like, and you bring up Daniel.* "Um, yeah. He's my ex. The guy who gave me the hat."

"I thought you said he moved away, and you weren't in touch?"

"Well, we're not, but it's complicated. Forget it."

"I can't now. Go on."

Staring into my mug of tea, I longed to jump in and disappear, but sensing my discomfort, Alex offered me an out. "Vic, I'm sorry, it's not my business. You don't have to tell me."

His words caused a tiny bit of trust to blossom, and I felt safe opening up. "It's okay, but promise me you won't laugh," I began. He nodded, so I continued. "I sometimes talk to his picture. I'm not crazy. He doesn't respond. But he's the first person who ever knew the real me, so sometimes saying things out loud to him helps me figure stuff out." Silence coated the room like a thick snowfall. "I swear to you, I'm not crazy. I also have Stephanie and Jenna to talk to, but I haven't had a chance yet."

"I don't think you're crazy," he said, his voice warm and reassuring. A few more seconds ticked by before I felt the heat of his hand on my back. "And the offer still stands. I'm here if you want to talk."

I needed to talk to someone about this, and thanks to his kindness, it was Alex. "Okay. The thing is, I'm kind of freaking out because I found out today that the art store might get sold. I'm finding it hard not to panic because I love it there, and the thought of not going there every day is upsetting. It's more than a job. I feel safe there, like I can be the real me. And Gunner can come, and I know our regular customers and the other shop owners nearby. It's great to be part of that community."

"That does sound good."

"Not good. Perfect. And I don't want it to end." I sounded like a child having a tantrum. "Sorry. I'm acting like a baby."

"Never apologize for your feelings," Alex said.

"Did you get that from a parenting book?"

"Maybe. But it's true. Here's another piece of wisdom. This one is from my gran. Don't trouble trouble until trouble troubles you. I guess I'm trying to say, don't worry until you know what will happen."

"I can't help it."

"Yeah. It's easier said than done." He placed a hand on my arm, causing a slight flutter in my stomach. "But you're smart and talented. And you have a good support network. Whatever happens, you'll get through it. And wow, I wanted to be helpful, not offer platitudes. Maybe talking to a picture is better after all."

This elicited a small smile from me.

"Okay, so I'm not so great at giving advice. But why don't we focus on the good stuff right now? Our cakes and designs were a hit. In fact, we hit it out of the ballpark."

"We did, didn't we?"

"I told you we're a good team."

"You were right," I agreed.

Surprising me, he reached over and grabbed my legs. I swiveled as he pulled my feet onto his lap. "If I can't help solve your problems, maybe I can help you relax. These hands are for more than creating mouth-watering delicacies," he said, wiggling his fingers before beginning to massage my feet.

"Oh, wow," I whispered, thinking that on one level, I should stop him, but the longing to be touched in an intimate, albeit innocent, way was too overwhelming.

"Just relax," he said.

I nodded and, closing my eyes, let out a contented sigh as his strong fingers worked their magic on my feet. The tension that had been building up inside me all day started to dissipate under his touch. I melted into the couch, my body sinking deeper and deeper into the soft cushions. And for the briefest moment, I felt that no matter what happened, I would be okay.

# 11

ALEX AND I WERE so busy over the next week that I didn't have time
to dwell on the potential sale of the art store. If neither of us had
full-time jobs enabling us to work on the cake full-time, it would
have only taken a couple of days, but we only had an hour or two
each evening, and it was taking me longer than I had estimated to
make the fondant forms of Jake and Stephanie. It was a medium I'd
only worked with briefly in the past, so I had to spend some time
learning its properties to mold and form it more effectively.

Before I knew it, it was the night of Stephanie and Jake's family
dinner, and we were at the restaurant three hours before Jake's family
was due to arrive. The restaurant's manager provided us with a small
area to assemble the cake and finish the last-minute details.

Alex had wanted to see how long it would take to assemble the
cake on site, pipe the borders, and add the figures. "You know what
the roads are like here, and while I'm sure a three-tier cake would
have been fine to transport, I'm thinking about the future—I'm not
sure if a six-layer cake could handle the journey. We'll use this cake
as an experiment to see how things go."

"Sure," I agreed. And while I knew we had plenty of time, I
couldn't stop my hands from shaking. At one point, Alex took mine
in his.

"Try to relax. It's all part of the learning process," he said. "And there's pretty much nothing icing can't fix."

"I know, but—"

"Trust me," he said. "It's cake. Not a nuclear bomb."

"It certainly feels that way," I said because the pressure was mounting. Not only did I want to make Stephanie happy, but Alex needed this for his business.

"How can I help you relax?" he asked.

"Talk to me. Tell me about yourself. Tell me why such a nice guy like you is divorced." The words slipped out because of my curiosity. Despite the closeness growing between us after a week of working together and sharing stories from our pasts, hc had yet to mention his ex-wife. He'd shared stories about where he'd grown up, his parents, his brother, and Noah, but not about his marriage.

"Straight for the jugular, huh?" A half-smile flickered across his face, one of both amusement and discomfort.

"I'm sorry. That was in poor taste. Why don't you tell me about your favorite hockey player instead?"

"No, it's fine, but I'm not sure this is the place." His gaze swept across the area where we worked. Then he shrugged. "I guess it's just us here."

With that, he took a deep breath and focused on piping the border around the base of the second tier. His expression changed to one of deep concentration, so I assumed he wasn't going to answer my question.

"We met when we were fifteen, and it was love at first sight," he said suddenly, switching piping bags. "We got married young, thinking we were unstoppable—this amazing couple getting ready to take on the world. We had plans and dreams and thought we could handle anything life threw at us. And we did for five amazing years. I completed my chef's training, and Simone earned a degree in communications. She'd just started at a community news show when we found out she was pregnant. We'd talked about starting a family once our careers were well established, so this was unexpected but also exciting. Pass me Jake, please."

The change of topic was so abrupt it took me a second to realize what he'd asked. I blinked, remembering the task at hand, and carefully passed him the fondant Jake.

He wiped perspiration from his brow with the back of his arm, then began placing Jake on the cake slowly and delicately. "Unfortunately, it was a difficult pregnancy," he began. "Simone had hyperemesis gravidarum. Essentially, it's severe morning sickness, and for Simone, it lasted the entire pregnancy. It's pretty uncommon, not that knowing that helped. She lost weight, was extremely tired, vomited several times a day, and fainted a few times while at work. She had to take medical leave, and basically, her life stalled for nine months. She was miserable, frustrated, and angry, and I don't blame her one bit."

I listened, feeling as if we were enveloped in a bubble that contained only us while the kitchen sounds of clanging pots and pans took place beyond, in a different world.

"It's time to put the tipped-over paint bucket on and run the icing down into the heart-shaped pool." He straightened up, having secured Jake in place, and there was a moment of contemplation, not only for the positioning of the figure but, I think, also for the chapter of his life he was sharing with me. He had revealed such a private and painful part of his past that I knew there were no words to express the depth of my sympathy. And I certainly didn't know how to convey my gratitude for his trust.

"Your turn," Alex said as he handed me the fondant bucket, his eyes lingering on my hands, which were no longer shaking. Now that I was able to place the bucket on the cake and pipe the puddle, I assumed he wouldn't share anything else. But I was wrong.

"The symptoms cleared up after Noah was born, but," he released a sigh, "Simone never really bonded with him. She was resentful that she'd missed such a great opportunity with her new job, and all that time in bed had her thinking about the future she wanted. Looking back, we both now believe that she had postpartum depression as well. But at the time, I didn't know how to help her. To me, Noah was the most beautiful, wonderful thing in the world, and I couldn't understand why she didn't seem to love him. Anyway, she hated breastfeeding, and after three months, we switched him to formula. After six months, she announced she was leaving." He moved closer and examined my work. "That looks great. Good job."

"Thank you," I replied to the compliment, hoping my voice carried an additional layer of thanks for his openness.

Alex's voice dropped to a softer tone. "I will spare you all the details about the emotional rollercoaster I rode for a year or two, but now Simone and I have a healthy relationship, and she is working on her relationship with Noah. I don't doubt that she loves him, but several years ago, I accepted that she doesn't want to mother him. Or be my wife."

"I'm so sorry," I whispered. "I don't know what to say."

A lopsided smile broke through his focused expression. "So, did my tale of heartache provide enough distraction?"

"You know it did. And thank you for sharing that with me." My words felt insufficient. There was so much more I wanted to express. I wanted him to understand that he could confide in me, rely on me, and count on me for support. Impulsively, I planted a lingering kiss on his cheek and hoped it spoke the words I failed to utter.

# 12

"I WASN'T FLIRTING," I argued, trying to keep my voice light as Stephanie, Jenna, and I sat in Stephanie's mother's kitchen eating pizza. I had just admitted to kissing Alex on the cheek, although I was careful not to reveal the subject of our conversation that led to it, merely describing it as serious. Alex had shared something very personal, and I wasn't about to break that newfound trust.

"Well, maybe not flirting because of the nature of your conversation, but it was definitely a sign of something," Steph corrected.

"We're friends. That's all. And so what if I find him attractive? I'm not going to act on it." My words sounded hollow, and I wondered if Stephanie and Jenna noticed. There were definitely moments when my attraction to Alex was so intense I wanted to give in to lust. His calming presence, his big blue eyes, and his playful smile drove me crazy with desire, especially when I tossed and turned late at night. And don't even get me started on his strong biceps and skilled hands when he worked in the kitchen. Then there was his loving demeanor toward Noah, his goofy jokes, his dedication to his job...it all just...whoa. I downed the rest of my pop. The trouble was, the more my attraction grew, so did my confusion.

"Why not?" asked Jenna.

"Why not what?" I asked, having completely lost my place in the conversation.

"Why not act on your attraction?"

"Well, because I don't know. I just won't."

"That's ridiculous," Stephanie and Jenna replied simultaneously.

"We're making cakes together. We have a good thing going, and I don't want to ruin it," I said.

"Or maybe you don't want to take a chance," Jenna said.

I shook my head. "We're a good team, and besides, what if—" I stopped myself, but not in time. There it was, bubbling to the surface: the never-ending question, the constant longing, the forever wondering.

"What if what?" Jenna asked.

"What if he's not interested?" I replied, hoping that would satisfy them, but Stephanie knew me too well. Her shoulder was the one I cried on when missing Daniel became overwhelming.

"Nice try. But that's not what you were going to say." Stephanie shook her head. "You were going to say, what if Daniel comes back?"

"No. Maybe. What if he does?"

Stephanie leaned across the table, wrapping her hands around mine. "Oh, sweetie, we've had this conversation more times than I can count. He's not coming back. You have to move on."

"How do you know?"

"Because it's been almost two years. If it was going to happen, it would have happened already. And besides, what's stopping you from going there? If you believed you should be together, you'd have flown to Hong Kong already."

Was she right? Probably. But asking me to move on was like asking me to give up on a dream.

"Personally, I think Vicki is afraid," Stephanie said, turning her attention to Jenna.

"Of what?" Jenna asked.

The pizza sat in my stomach like a stone. "Of being hurt. Of having to survive that kind of loss again," I mumbled.

Stephanie slapped her hand against the tabletop. "See. I was right."

"If that's the case, take it slow," Jenna said gently. "Whether he is Mr. Forever or Mr. Right Now, it doesn't matter. Just don't close the door on what could be amazing." She laughed and leaned into me, giving me a soft nudge. "Take what I say with a pinch of salt. It's not like I have a lot of experience."

"I think if it was purely physical, I would be okay with it. But I like Alex, and that makes me nervous," I admitted.

"Well, promise me this," Stephanie said. "He'll be your plus one at the wedding."

"What? Why?"

"He's going to be there anyway, delivering the cake, so ask him to stay. You need a date, and since you'll arrive together, he can be yours."

"That's so romantic," Jenna said sarcastically, and Stephanie stuck her tongue out at her.

"All right, Stephanie," Helen, Steph's mom, called out as she entered the kitchen. "I'm sorry to break up your hen party, but you're here for the dress fitting. Now, go make sure your hands and face are clean before trying on your dress. We're running out of time to get alterations done."

"But you're the one doing the alterations," Stephanie said.

"Yes, and I refuse to do them under duress mere hours before the wedding. Now let's go."

"Okay, fine," Stephanie exhaled dramatically but then wrapped her mom in an embrace, and a tiny part of me ached the way it sometimes did when I witnessed mother-daughter bonds. I loved my found family, but the sting of a mother's rejection cuts deep. I knew then that I had to steel myself for the emotions Stephanie's wedding was bound to evoke.

Perhaps Alex's presence could offer a distraction, a way to survive the day without getting too lost in thoughts of my past.

Stephanie returned five minutes later in a beautiful slim-fitting sequined gown with spaghetti straps and a slit on the side up to her mid-thigh.

"Steph, that's amazing," I said.

"Yeah, you look, wow, just wow," added Jenna.

Stephanie spun.

"Luckily, I think the only thing is to adjust the straps by about a quarter of an inch. That will bring up the bodice enough to give your tiny little boobs a bit of cleavage," Helen said.

"I see where you get your directness from, Steph," Jenna said, making us all laugh, especially Helen.

"What can I say? It's a family trait," Helen chuckled. "And as for you, my dear," she turned to me, "if you never risk your heart, you'll never know what could have been."

I replied with a nod, but my heart had been so battered I didn't know if there was any left to risk.

# 13

STEPHANIE'S WEDDING DAY ARRIVED in what felt like the blink of an eye. Alex and I had poured our hearts and souls into crafting the perfect cake, transforming my original sketch into a work of art that surpassed our wildest dreams. Knowing Stephanie would love it, I looked forward to stepping out of the kitchen and joining my friend in celebration.

But first, there were a few more details to attend to.

"Well, hello, gorgeous," Jenna said as I entered her kitchen. "You're stunning. New dress?"

"New to me," I said, curtseying in my latest thrift store find, a cayenne pepper red one-shoulder dress in velvet. "I'm glad you like it. And do you think you could zip me up?" I turned my back to her and held up my hair as her icy hands zipped me up. "Why thank you," I said. "I'm surprised Abby hasn't come running out. Is she not here?"

"No. She went with Matt to vacuum out the car. They'll be back soon."

"So, how do you want your hair?" I asked.

"I'm hoping you'll tell me that. My dress is black with a sweetheart neckline. Between Poppet and Abby, I don't want to put it on until the very last minute."

"Good idea." I took a step back and imagined different styles in my head. "Why don't we curl it and pin back the sides? I think it will look fabulous."

"If you say so." Jenna reached across the table and handed me a curling iron. I plugged it in and combed Jenna's hair before spraying it with a curl enhancer.

"So I have exciting news," Jenna said. "I've been picking up so many new clients recently that I'm thinking of hiring a part-time employee after Christmas."

"You're kidding. That's amazing. I'm so excited for you." It had been less than a year since Jenna started her mobile dog grooming business, and she worked extremely hard, so her success was well-earned. "Don't be surprised if I hand you my resume."

"What do you mean?" She attempted to turn her head to look at me, but I held the curling iron close to her ear.

"Don't move."

"Sorry, but you surprised me. What's wrong with your job? You love it."

"I know, but Isabelle mentioned the owner was considering selling the store."

"Oh no. But that doesn't mean it will close, does it?"

"No. But that also doesn't mean it won't. And even if it stays open, I probably won't be taking Gunner with me anymore. Most businesses don't want you to bring your dog to work." I released a sigh. "I was also excited about having extra money by occasionally working on cakes with Alex. So much for getting ahead. Now, everything is up in the air."

"That sucks. When do you think you'll know by?"

"That's the thing. I don't know. According to Isabelle, it's all up in the air. I've been so stressed since I found out. Luckily, I've had these cakes to work on. They've been a great distraction and have kept me sane." I took a deep breath and admitted the truth. "Alex's been a big help, too. He has a way of keeping me calm."

"Interesting. I bet he's been a very good distraction," she teased. "So it's safe to assume he's your plus one tonight?"

"Yes. He agreed to be with me at the front of the house, not only in the kitchen."

Jenna placed her hands over her heart. "It's like a fairy tale."

"Hey, be nice. Your hair is in my hands, and I have a weapon." I snapped the clamp of the curling iron.

"Good point," Jenna said. "Well, I, for one, am looking forward to meeting him. You've been spending a lot of time at his place."

"We were making a cake."

"Is that what they call it now?"

Before I could reply, Abby burst through the door. "Momma, Momma, we're back. We saw Daddy and Sylvanna. Her dress is blue. It's so pretty. I'm going to put mine on right now."

"Wash your hands and face first," Jenna called out. "Properly. With soap."

"I'm on it," Matt said, walking in and giving Jenna a quick kiss. "You look nice, Vic. Is the cake all ready?"

"Yeah. We were there all morning setting it up." Stephanie and Jake wanted it on display as the cake would be served early in the celebration, as there was no dinner, only cocktails and hors d'oeuvres. That way, we could string up the hanging leaves so they'd dance in the breeze above the cake. Suspended from the ceiling was a cheesecloth hammock holding more leaves, and Alex would pull a string when they cut the cake, and the hammock would release, allowing the leaves to fall. We must have tested it about ten times.

"I can't wait to try it," Matt said. "Oh, and I have a surprise for Abs. I picked up a dress for Poppet. I know the dog's not coming, but I thought we could get some pictures of Abby and Poppet before we go." He left to find Abby.

"I'm so lucky to have found him," Jenna whispered. "It still amazes me every morning when we wake up together."

I nodded. Matt had welcomed both Jenna and Abby into his heart. They were a package deal, and he never shied away from all that entailed, including having Josh move in across the hall.

Abby ran out in her pink dress. "Vicki, can you do my hair, too? Please, please, please?"

"There should be time," I told Abby, checking my watch. I was riding to the wedding with Alex, so I didn't want to be late. The thought of seeing him in formal attire, with his smile that could warm up the coldest autumn night, sent a bolt of excitement through me. We'd come to know each other, but only within one setting, the kitchen. Tonight, I'd see him in a different light, and the thought buzzed in my head that this would be a step toward new, uncharted territory in our relationship.

And surprisingly, I was eager to explore it.

Alex and I chatted with Jenna, Matt, Sylvanna, Josh, and Abby. Stephanie and Jake's house practically burst at the seams with guests, and the seven of us were crowded into the living room. Everyone eagerly awaited the bride and groom's arrival fresh from city hall. Abby bounced up and down, her eyes wide with excitement as Stephanie had given her a special job.

"They're almost here," a voice yelled from the kitchen, alerting us that the couple was about to arrive. We quickly made our way outside to line the walkway and welcome them home.

Grabbing Jenna's hand, Abby jumped up and down. "That's me. That's me. I have to do my job, Momma. Where's my basket of leaves?"

"By the front door, sweetie. Do you remember what to do?" Jenna asked.

"Of course." Abby turned to Josh. "Daddy, make sure you take my picture."

"Will do," Josh said, and Sylvanna passed him a camera out of her purse. "Thanks, Syl. Let's go."

Josh nodded at us, and then he and Sylvanna left with Abby.

"Should we all go outside now, too?" Matt asked.

"Absolutely," Jenna said, linking her arm through Matt's and leading the way.

As we headed outside, Alex reached for my hand and intertwined his fingers with mine. A mixture of excitement and comfort rushed through me, along with an overwhelming sensation of being wanted. My mouth went dry, and my stomach swirled with the frenzied flutter of a thousand butterflies. I found my heart dancing to the beat of the music that played in the background. Each pulse echoed the blissful realization that I was no longer the lone friend or the fifth wheel. With Alex by my side, my loneliness was gone. He caught my eye and smiled, and I imagined what it would be like if he never let go.

Lost in these thoughts, I walked beside Alex as we joined the other guests lining the walkway to the house. No one seemed to care about the chilly October day as the limousine drew up, and Jake stepped out to our applause. Then, he held out his hand for Stephanie. Even though I had already seen her in her dress, I gasped as she exited the limousine. Stephanie was stunning. She was always beautiful and well dressed, but today, an extra radiance emanated from within—the deep, soul-filling kind that comes from inside, from your heart.

I knew that feeling. I had experienced it with Daniel. But instead of becoming sad over what I had lost, I celebrated my dearest friend's love for Jake. That didn't stop a bittersweet tear from running down my cheek. But as I wiped it away, Alex squeezed my hand in reassurance, and I almost shed another tear at the relief and joy of having him by my side.

The crowd erupted into more cheers and applause as the happy couple walked past the guests, led by Abby, who tossed delicate fall leaves from her basket—leaves that Alex and I had cut from edible paper. Not only did they match the cake, setting the theme, but they would dissolve quickly in the snow, leaving no litter. That was all Alex's idea when I told him about Abby's job, and I had to admit, it was pretty genius, despite the blister on my thumb from all that cutting.

Once Jake and Stephanie reached the porch, they thanked everyone for coming, then ushered us all into the large heated tent in the backyard. Champagne bottles burst open, and the caterers greeted us with trays of delicious appetizers. The cake dominated one corner, a statement of love and celebration. The hanging leaves danced in the breeze, and Alex and I smiled at the oohs and aahs.

"I love how casual it all is," Alex commented as we were served hors d'oeuvres.

"Me too," I agreed. "If you had met Stephanie when she first moved into my building, you would have expected something big and flashy. But she's changed. She's figured out who she is now." I bit into a tiny quiche. "Plus, her band used to play at weddings often, and I think she tired of that scene. Although that's where she met Jake."

"Interesting," Alex mused. "I love getting to know your friends."

"Oh, yeah?"

"Yeah. You're lucky. Not everyone has such a wonderful group of friends."

"I am lucky," I agreed.

Jenna caught my eye from across the room, and then she and Matt wove through the crowd to join us.

"We were just admiring the cake," Jenna said.

"What do you think?" I asked.

"That it's crazy good," Matt exclaimed.

"Yeah, it's the most amazing cake I've ever seen," Jenna added. "No wonder you were so busy. And everything is edible? The leaves look real."

"That's Vicki's artistic skill. It blows me away," Alex said as he wrapped an arm around my waist and kissed the top of my head.

I felt Jenna's gaze and couldn't help but blush. "And it tastes better than it looks," I said, trying to deflect the attention. "You two are in for a treat."

Matt turned and glanced back at the cake. "We should probably go get Abby. We left her at the cake, and I think the temptation to sneak a piece of icing might eventually grow too strong for her to resist."

"Good idea," Jenna said, winking at me. "I know I couldn't resist if left alone."

I was wondering if her comment had double meaning as they walked away when Alex leaned in close, his breath caressing my cheek. "I told you it would work out."

"I hope so," I replied, wringing my hands nervously. "There's still the leaf drop."

"Which we practiced a dozen times."

"Not with the real leaves, though."

"I know, but here's the thing. Only the bride and groom know what to expect, and we prepared them for the possibility that it might not work. So, if it doesn't happen, no one but the four of us will know."

"Well, I won't relax until it's all done."

"Can I distract you with a dance?" he asked.

"You can try," I teased.

"Challenge accepted," he grinned, taking my hand and leading me to the crowded dance floor. As we swayed to the music, his hands settled comfortably on the small of my back, and I wrapped my arms around his neck.

He leaned his forehead against mine, and I nearly melted under the intensity of his gaze as he whispered, "I'm so glad we met."

My heart raced at his words, and despite the emotions clawing at my throat, I managed to reply, "Me too."

The music faded into a distant hum as the sound of blood rushing through my ears drowned out everything else. I liked this man—this man who looked like he wanted to kiss me and who I desperately wanted to kiss back.

As our gazes locked, he leaned in ever so slightly and brushed his lips against mine. The kiss was soft and tentative as if I were the most fragile thing on earth. Heat flushed through me, and my heart beat so fast that it felt like I'd run a marathon. I closed my eyes and leaned forward, signaling that I wanted more.

Alex leaned in with more force, and our touch ignited a fire we couldn't ignore. Then I remembered where I was, and Alex must have had the same realization because we drew apart.

He cleared his throat. "We should probably save that for later," he said, still holding me close.

"Absolutely," I agreed, and there wasn't a doubt in my mind that we'd have our own private dance later.

But for the time being, we continued around the dance floor until the slow song ended and an upbeat tune took its place. We reluctantly parted but continued to hold hands, not wanting to lose our connection. And in that instant, I decided to simply let go and enjoy the night with this man. Not the person who crafted the cake alongside me but my handsome, charming date who had captured a piece of my heart.

# 14

I awoke to Alex's gentle snoring, his body sprawled out beside mine. Holy moly. My mind reeled from the intensity of the night's events and the wild and intoxicating whirlwind that consumed us both. My body still hummed with pleasure and satisfaction. Together, we were a masterpiece, each moment a vibrant stroke of color, from the fiery red and orange passion that consumed us to the soft hues of blue and lavender that reflected our deep connection. His touch was like a paintbrush on my bare skin, leaving trails of desire and love in its wake.

I didn't want to leave his side, but the green glowing numbers of my alarm clock read nine o'clock, and reality set in. Jenna and I had hired a dog sitter for the evening, and Gunner had a sleepover with Poppet, but it was time to collect him. Alex would have to pick up Noah from his parents' place, too.

I kissed him gently on the cheek, then reluctantly drew back the sheets, but he reached out and pulled me back into his arms.

"Don't go," he murmured, his voice thick with sleep.

"I have to get Gunner. It's late."

"What time is it?"

"Nine."

"Wow," he chuckled. "You must have really tired me out. I can't remember the last time I slept until nine."

I swatted him playfully with a pillow.

"Please," he asked. "Five more minutes, and I'll get up with you."

"You're a hard man to say no to," I said, snuggling closer as he spooned me from behind. His hand traced down my side, stopping to rest on my hip. "I noticed your tattoo," he said, positioning his hand over it. "What is it? It was too dark last night for me to see it clearly."

Hesitation washed over me as I struggled to find the right words.

Perhaps I stiffened because Alex said, "You don't have to tell me if you don't want to," as if sensing my reluctance.

"I don't mind telling you. It's just hard to put into words all that it means." I took his hand from my hip and drew it to my lips, kissing his fingers. "The design is simple. It's the outline of Montreal with a heart in it. This is because Montreal is where I first felt truly loved and accepted. Whenever I'm overcome with self-doubt or insecurities, that tattoo and the one on my wrist remind me that I belong somewhere."

He drew my hand toward him and kissed my wrist tattoo. "Feel free to tell me to mind my own business, but are these reminders of your ex? The one whose picture you talk to?"

"Your pillow talk needs some work," I replied, trying to brush off the seriousness of his question. This wasn't a subject I wanted to embark on at the literal moment I found myself moving on from Daniel.

"It's just that, what with Noah and the way things ended with my ex-wife, I need to be careful with my heart," Alex continued. "Don't panic. I'm not saying we get married. I'm just saying that I like you, and I want to see where this takes us, but if you're still hung up on someone else, let me know now so we can still be friends."

His raw honesty was a sucker punch to my heart, so I rolled over to face him and spoke the truth. "I'll always love Daniel. He was my first love and taught me I was a person worthy of love and happiness. He changed my life by giving me the strength and the confidence to believe in myself." Taking a deep breath, I kept going. "Because things didn't end badly between us—our lives simply went in different directions—I have had a hard time letting him go, and to be completely honest, I've never had a reason to move on...until now." I met his gaze, hoping he would see my sincerity. "I want to see where this goes, too."

His earnest expression penetrated deep into my very soul. "I'm glad, and thank you for sharing that with me. But now, I kind of feel like a jerk for asking."

"Don't," I said. "I'm glad we both know where we're coming from."

He nodded, a small smile tugging at the corners of his mouth. Without hesitation, he pulled me in for a deep kiss. Immediately, sparks of desire ignited from within my body, but this kiss was layered with something beyond physical desire. A promise? A future? Whatever it was, I was ready to find out.

The shrill sound of the phone ringing shattered the moment. *Daniel?* Oh God. Why did I think that? I was in Alex's arms. The words that I was moving on had barely left my lips, but old habits die hard. Guilt washed over me before another thought jumped into my head. What if Gunner had gotten out?

I motioned to get up.

"Leave it," Alex said.

"I'm sorry, I can't," I said, untangling myself from his embrace and walking over to the phone. "Hello?"

"Yes, hello. Is this Vicki Meyers?"

"Speaking."

"Well, Miss Meyers, my name is Walter DiAngelo. I'm a lawyer in Ottawa hired by your mother, and I'm sorry to have to tell you this, but I'm afraid your mother has passed away."

His words cut through the beautiful morning like a knife. This had to be a mistake. My mother didn't even know where I lived. "My mother? You're sure?"

"Yes. I believe so. Sandy Meyers, born March 15, 1960."

That was definitely my mother's name and birthday. "Oh. Yes. That's her."

"I'm very sorry for your loss," Walter DiAngelo said.

My mouth went dry, and a boa constrictor made of painful memories wrapped around my chest and squeezed. I'd spent my teenage years preparing for this exact moment. Every night she didn't come home, I anxiously awaited a knock on the door or a phone call such as this. Yet, all these years later, I was completely unprepared.

My mother was dead.

"Miss Meyers, are you still there?"

Alex placed his warm hands on my shoulders, snapping me out of my thoughts.

"Yes. Sorry. It's just a lot."

Mr. DiAngelo took a deep breath. "Of course. Of course. And I won't keep you long. I know this must be a terrible shock, but at some point, soon, we do need to discuss your mother's will."

"My mother had a will?" Surprise mixed with confusion as I tried to comprehend what he'd said. My mother couldn't pay a bill on time or remember to buy groceries. When did she get a will?

"Indeed, she did. And there are some things we should discuss in person. I see you are in Montreal. Would it be possible for you to come to my office in Ottawa?"

"I guess," I heard myself replying, overriding the part of me that wanted to hang up and ignore the situation. Mom had never been there for me in life. Why should I be there for her in death?

"Great. When do you think you could make the trip?"

"I'm off on Wednesday."

"Wednesday? That works for me. Shall we say at eleven? That will give you plenty of time to get here. Do you have a pen and paper handy?"

I scribbled down the address, my hand shaking as I hung up the phone.

My mother was dead. And even though we hadn't spoken in years, a hole had been carved out of my heart.

Still naked, I collapsed onto a kitchen chair. Alex picked up a blanket from the bed and wrapped it around me. He was getting me a glass of water when there was a knock on the door.

"One minute," he said, and I heard him fumbling with his pants. He opened the door and stepped into the hall. I heard a muffled conversation before Alex returned. "Matt and Abby are taking Gunner and Poppy for a walk."

"Poppet," I snapped.

"What?"

"The dog's name is Poppet."

"Oh. Sorry."

"No. I'm sorry. It's just that...my mother's dead."

He pulled out the other chair and sat beside me. "I heard. I'm so sorry."

"And they need me in Ottawa. Something to do with the will."

He nodded. "Are you okay? Other than telling me about her alcohol addiction, you've never really spoken about your mother."

"It's hard to speak about her. I haven't seen her for years. She got knocked up at fifteen, and her parents kicked her out. I don't know why she didn't give me up for adoption, but she didn't. She coped by turning to drugs and alcohol. My childhood was...challenging."

"Jesus, Vicki." He reached out and wrapped an arm around me. "I can't imagine how complicated your feelings must be right now."

"Yes, yes, that's exactly it. I don't know what to feel. I don't know what to think." Then I collapsed against him and cried. "Leaving home was the best decision I ever made, but part of me always hoped my mother would reach out one day. I told myself it was better she never did because she'd probably ask for money, but I always clung to the hope of reconciliation. I thought about finding her a few years ago, but I wasn't strong enough. But I have been for a while, and maybe I should have looked for her. Maybe then she wouldn't be dead."

"Hey, Vic, it's not your fault," Alex soothed.

"I know, I know. But still..." I grabbed a tissue and wiped my nose. "Now it's too late. I'll never know if she loved me. I've been robbed of the chance to find out." My heart ached with regret.

A fresh wave of sobs overtook me as I struggled to compose myself. Despite my efforts, my body continued to shake and tremble. In a daze, I grabbed some sweats and a T-shirt and began making tea.

"Here, let me." Alex's calm voice broke through my turmoil as he gently took the kettle from my shaking hand. He put the kettle on, then picked up the phone. "Do you mind if I call my parents to let them know I'll be late picking up Noah?"

About to tell him to go ahead, I changed my mind. I wanted him with me. I needed him with me. But the intensity of those feelings scared me and I panicked. "Don't change your plans. I'll be okay."

"I can't leave you."

"I'll be fine," I argued. "Besides, Jenna and Matt are around if I need anything."

"I don't feel right about it."

"Please, Alex, go. I need to be alone for a while." It was better that way. Having him near added more conflict to my already chaotic mind because part of me desperately wanted him to stay and hold me, but another part feared the intensity of our connection. Things were too new between us, and the thought of being so exposed and vulnerable in front of him was overwhelming. Pushing him away was easier.

# 15

THE DAYS BETWEEN WALTER DiAngelo's phone call and the Wednesday of our appointment were endless. Sleep eluded me as my mind raced with questions, guilt, and uncertainty. My shifts at work dragged on as each minute unfolded like an eternity as I waited for the inevitable meeting in Ottawa.

I longed to call Stephanie for a shoulder to cry on and some blunt advice, but I couldn't bring myself to interrupt her honeymoon. Luckily, I had support from both Jenna and Alex—yes Alex, despite my initial reaction of pushing him away I found myself craving his company. They even joined me on the trip to Ottawa.

Alex drove while I stared blankly out the window. Jenna sat behind me, and the only sound in the car came from a Neil Diamond album that was stuck in the CD player. I chided myself for being so affected by my mother's death. Yes, it was an enormous shock, but her loss would have no effect on my life. My life had been better without her in it, and I wondered if I was mourning her or if I was mourning the loss of hope for a future where we'd reconnect. Maybe both, but it's not that it mattered, as I'd likely never figure that out.

When I left home all those years ago, I was insecure, unloved, and alone. The desperation for affection resulted in my relationship with Kent, and the mere thought of opening old wounds terrified me. I wouldn't do it—I couldn't do it. So, when I awoke on Wednesday, I convinced myself that once I got through the day, I'd process my grief as best I could and then return to my normal life.

"We're here," Alex announced, pulling into the parking lot of a small office building on the outskirts of town. He turned off the engine, and we sat in silence, all eyes fixed on the unassuming building before us.

"Okay, let's get this over with," I muttered, opening my door and stepping out into the cold, windy morning.

Jenna wrapped an arm around my shoulder. "We're here for you. Don't worry."

I nodded in response.

We entered the building and climbed the stairs to the second floor, where Walter DiAngelo's office was located. As soon as we entered the reception area, a tall man with salt and pepper hair and a bushy mustache appeared from an adjoining room.

"Good morning," he said, greeting us with a welcoming smile. "I'm Walter DiAngelo, but please, call me Walter."

"I'm Vicki Meyers," I began, struggling to keep my voice steady. "And these are my friends, Alex and Jenna."

Walter shook our hands one by one. "Ah, well, good for you for bringing reinforcements. This is an emotional time, and it helps to have people to lean on."

"Yes," I agreed.

"Since there are four of us, let's go into the conference room instead of my office. After you," Walter said, motioning toward the door on our left. "I just have to retrieve your mother's file, and I'll be right in."

With a sinking feeling in my stomach, I entered the room where my past and present were about to collide.

We settled into our seats around an oval table and waited for Walter to begin. He sat across from me, cleared his throat, and interlaced his fingers on top of a legal-sized manilla folder. "Thank you for coming. As you've come such a long way, and there is much to discuss, let's get down to business."

*Much to discuss? How could the will of a destitute addict have much to discuss?*

"Your mother drafted this will a couple of years ago and entrusted me to contact you should the need arise. Please know that Sandy planned on contacting you herself at some point, but unfortunately, that day never came."

My heart clenched as I struggled to process his words. "She what?"

He gave me a small smile. "I'm not privy to all the details of your past together, but I do know the two of you were estranged and that one day, your mother hoped to rectify that."

His words spun before me, sucking the air from the room like a black hole. I couldn't breathe. This was too much to bear. The revelation that she wanted to find me but hadn't yet reached out was worse than not knowing at all. It was like holding onto a winning lottery ticket only to have it ripped away seconds later.

Alex squeezed my knee, breaking through my shock. "You okay?"

"I don't know." The emotions swirling inside me threatened to spill over and drown me in a tidal wave of grief and confusion. I resorted to my bad habit of chewing on the inside of my cheek as I desperately tried to hold myself together.

"I'm sorry this is such a shock, but I'm not surprised," Walter said, his voice calm. "Sandy never hid her troubled past."

The world sat heavily on my chest. On my heart. "Did you know her well?"

"Not well, but we were friends. We met at AA."

"AA? You met at AA?" My voice raised an octave, and I leaned forward, incredulous. "You mean she got sober?"

"Yes," Walter confirmed. "And the reason I'm being open about it is because she wanted you to know."

"So why didn't she tell me herself?"

"Everyone goes through the steps at their own pace."

Anger burned in my throat. She got sober and wanted to reach out. But then she died. It wasn't fair. None of this was fair.

Walter stared at his hands for a few seconds before continuing. "So, the reason I asked you to come to my office instead of simply informing you of the situation via phone call is so that we can get the paperwork handled promptly. Your mother made you the beneficiary of her life insurance pol—"

"Life insurance policy?" I blurted. "She had freaking life insurance, too?"

"She did," Walter replied in his ever-calm voice.

I collapsed against the back of my chair, completely stunned. The woman Walter knew and the woman who raised me were two completely different people. "This is a lot to take in."

"It is. Would you like a glass of water?"

"No, I'm okay. Please continue."

"As I was saying, your mother listed you as a beneficiary on her life insurance policy. The payout is modest, and a large portion covered her cremation expenses. However, there is still some left for..." He closed his eyes briefly as if steeling himself before delivering more bad news. Immediately, I assumed my mother had accumulated some debt and he was about to inform me that the remainder of her life insurance would cover it. Then a worse thought entered my mind—what if he was preparing to tell me that I would be liable for her outstanding debts. I braced myself for what was to come.

He opened his eyes, locking his gaze onto mine. "There is still some left for you and your sister."

# 16

"SISTER?" I YELLED OUT as his words hit me like a physical blow. Nothing in a million years could have prepared me for the bombshell Walter had dropped. "There must be some kind of mistake. I don't have a sister."

Walter's gaze remained steady, and his mouth was set in a line of unwavering calm. "When was the last time you saw your mother?"

"I don't know. About eight years ago, I guess."

"Right. Well, a lot can happen in that time." His poised expression never faltered. But then, why would it? He was merely the messenger, delivering blow after blow of life-altering news. "And you do indeed have a sister. Her name is Lucy, and she's three, and your mother has named you her legal guardian."

I stood so fast my chair tipped over. "Are you kidding me? Why would she do that? She doesn't even know me."

Alex leaned down to pick it up when I turned to race for the door. I tripped over his arm and landed on the floor.

Both Alex and Jenna jumped up to help me, but I held up my hand, signaling stop. "No. Don't." I stood and brushed off my knees. "Wait here. Both of you. I need to be alone." With that, I bolted from the building, my legs shaking uncontrollably as I ran.

I reached the edge of the parking lot before stopping to sit on a curb. My head throbbed, unable to control the tornado of questions, emotions, and childhood memories that whirled within it. *Was this really happening? A sister? My sister?*

I'm not sure how long I sat there before Alex appeared beside me, his shadow long and lean from the low winter sun. Without a word, he sat beside me and wrapped his arms around me in a silent, comforting embrace.

It was exactly what I needed.

"This is a lot of baggage to unpack," I said softly before suddenly sobbing against his chest.

Alex tightened his embrace and planted a soothing kiss on the top of my head.

"It's so unfair," I said against his chest, choking out the words as I tried to stifle my sobs. "When I was young, I dreamed about having a brother or sister, so I wouldn't be alone. But as I grew older, I realized it was better to be alone than to have someone else suffer like I did. And now, not only do I find out that I have a sister, but that sister had a sober and present mother, and I can't help but wonder why my mother couldn't get sober for me." I took some deep breaths in an effort to quell the rise of more sobs. "I'm confused, hurt, angry, excited, and even a bit jealous. Oh, and scared. I'm very, very scared."

"I can't even begin to imagine what you're going through right now," Alex said. "All I can do is remind you that you don't have to go through it alone. You have me, and you have your friends. We'll all be there for you."

I knew without a doubt Jenna and Stephanie would be by my side, but Alex? My life had suddenly become very messy for someone who was just getting to know me. Our relationship was new; it should have been fun and exciting, not bogged down by the ghosts from my past. And not only ghosts. A living, breathing sister.

"We should probably head back in," I murmured after a moment.

"Whenever you're ready," he reassured me.

I nodded in agreement, but a thought lingered in my mind: what if I was never ready?

Once again, we were gathered around the conference room table, listening to Walter explain the role of guardian. All that crying had left my eyes puffy and my face blotchy, but it had been both necessary and cathartic. Although I would need more time to fully process the reality of my new situation, I felt composed enough to focus on the practicalities—not that I had a choice.

"I'm confused. The guardianship is temporary?" asked Jenna.

"Yes and no," Walter replied. "Because Vicki was named in the will, she is granted custody of the child for ninety days. If she wants to keep her, then she needs to apply for permanent guardianship, and, so long as things are going well, the court will grant her permanent custody."

"And what happens if I don't want custody or I can't handle it?" I asked. "I don't know what it's like to care for a child."

"Then it's up to the court to decide what's in the child's best interest."

A lump formed in my throat. "By which you mean Lucy would go into foster care."

Walter's nod was solemn. "Yes, and hopefully, she would eventually find a loving family through adoption."

The vivid image of Gunner alone in his pen at the animal shelter popped into my head. I pictured him huddled in the corner. His head hung low, and his eyes brimmed with a deep, inconsolable sadness. The sense of dejection had been palpable. Could I subject any child to a similar fate, let alone my sister? Of course not. "Wow. No pressure," I said, letting out a weary sigh.

"Listen, Vicki, you don't have to make all the decisions today. I would never ask you to do that, especially since I blindsided you." Walter smiled apologetically. "Based on my experience, the best course of action is to take it one step at a time. For now, this situation is temporary. Ninety days. That will give you time to adjust and think about the future. In the meantime, we'll book your court case, and as that day approaches, you can decide the best course of action for both you and the child."

"But I take Lucy home with me today?"

"If possible, yes."

"What about the father?" Alex asked. "Does he have a role in Lucy's life? And if so, will that be an issue for Vicki now or in the future?"

Thank goodness Alex was there to ask such a crucial question. Having grown accustomed to my mom's single status, the thought of having a father in the picture never occurred to me, especially given my mother's less-than-stellar track record with men. The long list of losers she used to bring home marched through my mind. Surely, no court would place a child with any of those men.

Walter was quick to respond. "As far as I know, no father is in the picture, and I believe only your mother's name is on Lucy's birth certificate."

"That's good," I said, then worrying I'd insulted Alex, I began stumbling over my words. "I don't mean that in the sense that not having a father is good. I mean that because I was named guardian, there won't be a custody battle. It's more straightforward. Besides, my mom always dated jerks. But if Lucy has a father who wants to be involved—"

Alex placed a comforting hand on my shoulder. "I get it, Vic. Don't worry."

I nodded in relief. "So where is Lucy now?" I stupidly glanced around the room as if she'd been there the entire time, hiding under a table or something.

"At home with your mother's roommate," Walter said, picking up a pen and flipping through his folder. "We can go there now. I will accompany you and provide the introductions to Bonnie so you can follow me, but I'll give you the address in case we get separated."

The address. The introduction. This was it. A countdown clock to sisterhood began in my head. "Yeah. Okay. Great. I should go meet her, shouldn't I? Wait. No. Sorry. That's a stupid question because I have to do more than that, right? Not only am I meeting her, she's coming to live with me. Oh my God. Where will she sleep? What if she's allergic to dogs? What if she hates dogs? What if she hates me?"

"Easy, Vic," Alex said.

"We'll have the drive home to figure things out," Jenna added. "So, no need to panic."

A laugh tinged with irony slipped out. Panicking seemed like a viable option to me. But the word home planted itself in my brain. Home. The very thought of my apartment, my dog, and my tea helped collect my scattered thoughts and provide a sense of direction. I needed to get home.

But first I had to meet my sister.

# 17

We followed Walter, and the familiar streets of my hometown passed by. Since moving to Montreal, I never once felt homesick for this place. This city was tainted with nothing but painful memories.

After about fifteen minutes, we arrived at a small lowrise building in a different part of town from where I'd grown up.

Walter led us down a narrow hallway to an end unit on the first floor. While the building showed signs of wear and tear, the paint on the walls was fresh, and someone had recently mopped the floors, which was already an improvement compared to our old apartment.

Walter knocked, and the door immediately swung open. I was surprised by the ceiling height and the streams of sunlight pouring through the large living room window. Furnished sparsely with mismatched pieces, it was clean and organized—a level of comfort far beyond anything my mother and I experienced together.

A petite woman with a cigarette in her hand stepped back from the doorway and welcomed us into her home. From her appearance, I guessed her to be in her forties or fifties, though it was hard to tell as years of smoking had left heavy wrinkles on her face. Her eyes glistened with tears as she approached me, wrapping me in an unexpected hug. Her dry, blond hair tickled my face, and her teeth were notably yellow when she pulled away from me and smiled.

"Oh, honey, you look exactly like your mother. I'd have recognized you anywhere," she said warmly.

I didn't know how to reply to that. 'Thank you' seemed wrong after spending my entire life trying not to resemble the woman who barely raised me.

"Vicki, this is Bonnie, your mother's roommate," Walter said. And Bonnie, you seem to have figured out who Vicki is, so let me introduce you to Jenna and Alex, her friends from Montreal."

"How nice to meet you all. I'm just sorry it had to be under these circumstances. Now, come on in and sit down. Walter and I have some things to discuss, and then I'll wake Lucy up from her nap."

I nodded, feeling Alex's hand on my back guiding me toward a three-seater sofa. The living room was a bright space open to the kitchen. As I moved to sit down, I noticed the fridge was covered in photos. Without thinking twice, I crossed the room, unable to resist a glimpse into my mom's life.

While I had no pictures from my childhood, the fridge was plastered with ones of my sister. My mother was in some, as was Bonnie—everyone smiling as they sat around a birthday cake, walked along the canal, and played at a park. Moments like these never existed in my childhood, and a deep ache settled in my chest. I wondered if this could have been my life had Mom been sober.

And then I saw it. A picture of me was in the top right corner. *What the hell?* I snatched it off the fridge. It was a photo from a fundraising event for the animal shelter.

Bonnie's voice startled me. "She printed that off the internet. Finding out that you were happy and doing well lifted a huge weight off her shoulders. She was so afraid she'd ruined your life. But after finding that, she smiled a lot more."

"How did she get it?" Stunned, my voice was barely more than a whisper.

"We made some friends at rehab who are good with computers. They tracked you down for her."

The lump in my throat felt as big as the moon. My mother had known where I lived. "Didn't she want to contact me?"

"Of course she did, honey. But she was nervous. Your mom carried a lot of shame from the old days and wasn't ready yet. She wanted to make you proud, but she also needed to be strong enough in case you rejected her. She was getting there. But then—" Bonnie's voice cracked. "But then she ran out of time."

I placed the photo back on the fridge with shaking fingers. "I need to sit down."

I stumbled back toward the couch, sitting beside Alex, who wrapped his arm around me. I took some deep breaths to steady the chaos swirling inside me. The urge to escape, to flee back to Montreal, was overwhelming. I wanted to run right out of that building and not stop until I reached the top of Mount Royal. I'd tell my troubles to Daniel, and from our special spot, the wind would carry them across the vast 8000-mile chasm. My body ached with a deep, visceral yearning for him, for the familiar comfort only he could provide.

Alex's arm tightened around me reassuringly, but instead of finding comfort, I stiffened. While I liked him, thinking I could move on after Daniel had been a mistake. Daniel was the only person I needed. This realization caused me to withdraw into myself, and I deflated like a leaky balloon.

Walter began speaking, but his words were distant and muted as he handed me a card that I couldn't bring myself to accept. When I didn't react, Alex reached for it, and I watched Walter exit the apartment as if he hadn't completely altered the course of my life.

Bonnie offered me a glass of water, which I eagerly accepted. Each sip sent an icy chill down my throat, numbing the chaos in my mind and giving me the strength to face what was to come. I needed to gather the scattered pieces of my mind. I was a twenty-six-year-old woman, not a child, and the time had come to accept my new reality.

"Oh, I think I hear Lucy stirring. I'll be one second," Bonnie said, disappearing into another room.

"Ready for this?" Alex whispered, and Jenna squeezed my knee.

I nodded. The question of my mother's love had haunted me all my life. Now, with the revelation that she searched for me and wanted to make amends, a long-broken part of my heart began to mend, stitching together pieces I thought were lost forever.

I would do this for my sister, whose world depended on me now. I would do it for my mother, who finally found the strength to change her life, and I would do it for myself because I'd been given an amazing gift—a sister.

So yes, I was ready.

Bonnie returned a few minutes later carrying a tiny child. Lucy. Her head nestled against Bonnie's neck.

"Lucy," Bonnie said gently as she sat in an armchair, "I have someone I'd like you to meet. This is Vicki. She's your sister."

Lucy turned to me shyly, rubbing her eyes and sticking her thumb in her mouth. The family resemblance was striking, much more noticeable in person than in the pictures on the fridge. Her eyes were wide, filled with uncertainty, starkly contrasting the happy child in the photos. My heart broke open, and love for my sister poured out, welcoming her into my life. I would do everything I could to give her a good home.

"Hi," I said, reaching out to touch her tiny hand. "It's nice to meet you. And these are my friends. Alex and Jenna."

"Hi there," Alex said.

"Hi," said Jenna.

Lucy continued to stare.

"Remember how we talked about your sister who lived in Montreal?" Bonnie asked. "And that you might get to go live with her?"

Lucy nodded.

"Good, because Vicki's here to take you home with her."

"Want Mommy," Lucy said.

Bonnie closed her eyes in a long blink as tears welled up in mine. "Your mom's gone, sweety. Remember how Mommy was sick and couldn't get better? She told you she'd made sure there was someone to take care of you and for you not to be afraid."

"Stay here," Lucy said.

"I'm going to miss you too," Bonnie said, placing a kiss on Lucy's forehead. "But I can't take care of you. Vicki can. She's blood. She's your sister."

"I am," I said, desperately wanting to ease some of Lucy's pain and confusion. "I lived with Mom until I was almost eighteen years old." There was no need to admit I'd been desperate to leave. That I could no longer live with her indifference. That I was terrified I'd come home one day to find our mother dead from an overdose or abusive boyfriend or that one day she might not come home at all. None of that would make sense to Lucy because the mother who raised her was not the one who raised me.

Her uncertain expression wasn't all that different from the look on Gunner's face when I'd first met him at the animal shelter. It took some time, but finally, he trusted me. I imagined a similar process with Lucy.

"Vicki's an artist," Jenna said. "She draws pictures for my daughter to color in. Do you like to color?"

Lucy nodded.

"Great. I bet she'd draw one for you when we get home."

"Oh, absolutely," I said. "Do you like dogs? I'm good at drawing my dog, Gunner. I could draw you a picture of him. He's gray and white, but you can color him any color you want. Well, not him, but the picture. You get what I mean, don't you?" I chewed on the inside of my cheek.

"And you'll like our house," Jenna added. "I live in the apartment upstairs with my daughter, Abby. She just turned five."

"And my son is three as well, so there are lots of kids for you to play with," Alex said.

Bonnie placed Lucy on the floor. "I have to get to work soon, sweetie, and I'm sure you want to see your new home. Why don't you show Alex and Jenna your room so they can help you gather your things if that's okay with them," Bonnie asked, turning to Jenna. "I need to talk to Vicki for a moment."

Jenna stood. "No problem."

The three of them left the room, leaving Bonnie and me alone.

"We can talk in the kitchen. I need to make a snack before leaving for work," she said.

I followed her and waited while she popped some bread into the toaster. "I'm sure there's a lot you want to know, so I'm just going to talk, and hopefully, it fills in some of the blanks. Let's start with Lucy." Bonnie reached for a cigarette but didn't light it. "I didn't meet your mom until after she was pregnant. If she knew who the father was, she never mentioned a name to me. Even sober, she had terrible taste in men," Bonnie said, chuckling softly. "She was in a bad way and living on the street when she realized she was pregnant, but it was her wake-up call. She told me that she vowed to get clean as soon as she found out. That's when I met her. We were in the same rehab facility. She was such a frail little thing. And terrified. But so determined to do things right. She never forgave herself for how you grew up. That was the hardest thing for her to live with in sobriety. How she hurt you."

I took a moment to let this information sink in. Though nothing could erase the painful memories of my childhood, knowing that my mother acknowledged her mistakes was a comfort. "I'm glad she got her life sorted out, but that doesn't explain why she made me guardian of her child without contacting me first." I tapped the picture of me on the fridge. "Obviously, she knew where I was."

"I know. But recovery is complicated and tough. She feared you'd reject her, just as her parents did when they found out she was pregnant with you. And if that happened, she was terrified she'd relapse. Just know that she wanted to. Every day, she was growing stronger. She even went to Montreal a few months ago but couldn't bring herself to do it. Then she got sick and, well...here we are."

"She was sick?" When Walter had first called, I'd been so certain she'd died of an overdose I never thought to ask. And then, thanks to the avalanche of all the other shocking details about my mother's life, that question got buried. "How did she die?"

"Pneumonia." Bonnie's voice cracked as she placed her toast slices on a plate and began spreading them with peanut butter. "She thought it was a terrible cold. We both did. But it kept getting worse, and by the time I convinced her to go to the hospital, it was too late." Bonnie wiped away some tears. "And before your mind goes there, it wasn't from AIDS. Your mother didn't inject drugs. The doctor told me that the infection simply overtook her immune system."

Emotion clogged my throat. My mother and I had been so close to reconnecting. So darn close. A pang of regret hit me, causing me to wonder what would have happened if I had stayed in Ottawa. But that thought was fleeting. The decision to leave my mother and eventually move away from Ottawa had been for the best. I had to save myself, just as my mother eventually saved herself. And as it turned out, we'd both succeeded. Perhaps the Meyers women were strong after all.

If only I could have told her that.

"Are you okay?" Bonnie asked.

I gave her a warm smile. This had been a hell of a day, but I was pulling myself together and gaining strength. "I should be asking you the same thing."

Bonnie leaned against the sink and sighed. "I'll be okay," she finally said, rinsing her plate. "I miss your mother with all my heart, and I'll miss the little one, too, but this is what Sandy wanted. And as much as I love Lucy, I can't raise a child." She looked at me with pleading eyes. "Just promise me you'll keep in touch. I'd love to know how Lucy's doing and if you ever want to talk about Sandy..." Her voice trailed off.

"Of course," I promised.

Bonnie pulled me into a tight embrace. Her tears wet my shoulder as she whispered, "Well then, I guess I better say goodbye to Lucy and let you take her home." She pulled away and wiped her eyes. "I'm sorry, but sometimes doing the right thing hurts."

I traced the tattoo on my wrist, knowing exactly how right Bonnie was.

# 18

As the car rolled to a stop in front of our building, I sighed in relief. All I wanted was to hug Gunner and make a cup of tea. But there would be no relaxing. My days of curling up on the futon with Gunner to draw or daydream had vanished in the blink of an eye, and I allowed myself to feel a tiny bit of resentment. I had gone to Ottawa, assuming all I had to do was fill in some paperwork, and I'd returned with a dependent. A sister.

"Lucy," I whispered, touching her arm to wake her. "We're here. It's time to get out of the car."

She rubbed her eyes and immediately stuck her thumb in her mouth, a habit I knew would need correcting, but not today. If it helped her relax, so be it.

Alex opened Lucy's door and helped her out of the car seat. "Here, kiddo, I'll help you," he said kindly as he took her small hand in his. They walked around the car together and joined me on the sidewalk.

"This is where I live," I told Lucy, pointing to the first-floor apartment with the large window. "Jenna lives upstairs, and Alex and his son Noah live next door. That's how we know each other. My dog, Gunner, is in Jenna's apartment with Jenna's dog, Poppet. They're friends, too. Oh, and Jenna will introduce you to Abby later. I bet you, Noah, and Abby will also become fast friends."

She looked up at me with big, confused eyes.

Poor kid. Talk about information overload.

I smiled at her, hoping she couldn't see the fear in my eyes. Were kids like dogs? Able to sense fear? I hoped not.

"It's getting late, and I'm starving," Jenna said. "I'm going upstairs and will have Matt order us a pizza. Why don't the two of you come up in about half an hour? We can all have dinner together, and Lucy can meet Abby. Alex, did you want to join us?"

"I'd love to, but I need to pick up Noah from my parent's place." He leaned down and kissed my cheek before heading off. "I hate to leave you, but I feel good leaving you in Jenna's care."

"Thank you for your help today."

"That's what friends are for, right?"

I nodded. Friends. How things had changed since Sunday morning. He must have picked up on my discomfort at Bonnie's place when I thought of Daniel. Or maybe starting a relationship with me now that I was responsible for Lucy was more than he wanted. He already had a child and was busy enough. I couldn't blame him for wanting distance. In fact, I was relieved.

Several minutes later, I was alone with Lucy for the first time. I knew if I didn't keep busy, I'd have an anxiety attack. "Let's get you a place where we can put your things. I have a big closet, so we'll put your clothes in there." I opened the closet and emptied the lowest shelf for Lucy's suitcase. "We can unpack it later and see what you have. Bonnie gave us a box of toys. Let's open that." I placed the box in front of Lucy. "Do you have a favorite toy?"

Lucy's nod was slight but eager, her small hand reaching into the box. She pulled out a plush bear with fur as blue as the summer sky, its embroidered eyes bright and cheerful. She hugged it tightly to her chest, and for the first time, I noticed a hint of a smile on her lips.

"Does he have a name?" I asked.

"Bluey," Lucy said.

"Well, hi there, Bluey; welcome to my home." I shook one of Bluey's paws, and Lucy let out a small giggle.

Before long, we went upstairs to Jenna's apartment. Gunner was happy to see me, and I gave him a big hug. He then sniffed Lucy and plopped onto the floor, rolling onto his side.

"He wants you to rub his belly," I told Lucy. "Like this." I squatted down and scratched his tummy. Lucy followed suit and gently touched the dog's tummy. Gunner's tail thumped on the floor.

"See, he likes it," I said. She squealed in delight and laughed when he licked her hand. Abby heard her and came out of her room with Poppet. Soon, Abby, Lucy, and the two dogs were playing in Abby's room.

By the time we finished the pizza and returned to my apartment, I was ready to fall asleep. Both Lucy and I changed into our pajamas, brushed our teeth, and climbed into bed. Lucy slept in the sleeping bag Abby loaned her. I took the other side of the bed, petting Gunner, who slept on the floor beside me. As I drifted off to sleep, I saw myself as a child of maybe six or seven, sitting at the table. In front of me sat a glass of water and a bowl of cold animal pasta. My mother was out somewhere getting high. Lonely and scared, I remember wishing for a brother or sister so I wouldn't have to be alone anymore.

Twenty years too late, my wish had come true.

# 19

I COULDN'T REMEMBER IF I'd ever been so tired. It wasn't only physical exhaustion—my mind had been running a mental marathon. Ever since that phone call from Walter DiAngelo, my life had changed at lightning speed, and keeping up with everything proved a bigger challenge than I'd ever imagined.

"Would you like some juice?" I asked Lucy, who sat on the futon dressing Bluey. She nodded and slid off the futon, climbing into her booster seat at the table. She didn't talk much or smile often. Not that I could blame her, but at what point should I become concerned? How do I find a pediatrician? How do I get her old medical records? There was no end of things to do or worry about.

"Here you go," I said, placing a juice box before her. I poured myself some tea and sat across from her. Oh, how I longed to crawl inside my teacup and bathe in relaxing chamomile. Not that there was time. Isabelle had given me nearly two weeks off, and I had used every second to toddler-proof my apartment and research toddler-friendly foods. Then Jenna helped me tour the daycare center, where she sent Abby, and I enrolled Lucy. We'd also gone shopping for new winter clothes and boots.

But amidst all this chaos, my mind occasionally thought of Alex. We'd spent so much time together in the past month that more than a week without him seemed odd. It was Sunday afternoon; he wasn't working.

"I have an idea," I said to Lucy. "Let's take Gunner for a walk and go to the park." I picked up the phone and dialed Alex's number before I could second-guess myself. He answered, his voice warm and familiar, and he agreed to accompany us to the park.

We bundled up in layers, and Gunner's booties got a laugh out of Lucy. We'd received about two inches of snow, so I was a bit concerned about what there would be to do at the park, but even if we turned around, the fresh air would be stimulating in and of itself. Gunner was happily sniffing around and marking every shrub in sight when Alex and Noah joined us on the sidewalk.

"Well, if it isn't my favorite neighbor," Alex said, squatting down to pet Gunner.

"Hey," I replied with mock annoyance. "Thanks a lot."

He chuckled and turned his attention to Lucy. "And how are you, Miss Lucy?"

Lucy looked at the ground and stuck her thumb in her mouth.

"This is my son, Noah," Alex continued. "He's about your age."

Neither child said anything.

"All right, well, shall we?" Alex stood, then made a dramatic bow and ushered me forward with a sweep of his arm. "I was happy to hear from you this morning," he said, lacing his fingers with mine. "I've missed you. I would have called you myself, but I wanted to give you time to get settled."

I missed you too, lodged in my throat. Unable to respond, I simply gave his hand a squeeze. Guilt over longing for Daniel prevented me from uttering those words to this thoughtful man. If I liked Alex as much as I thought, I didn't understand why I only wanted Daniel's presence in

Ottawa. I had to wonder if I was lonely and using Alex to fill a void in my life. I shouldn't have invited him to join us. My feelings were too conflicted, raising questions I didn't have time for. My priority had to be Lucy and nothing else.

"How's it going, anyway?" he asked, apparently satisfied with the hand squeeze.

"I'm tired and overwhelmed," I admitted. "Luckily, I've been off work. It's given me time to get organized. Tomorrow is my first day back."

"Well, good luck. And don't hesitate to call me, night or day."

"Thanks, but I need to figure things out on my own."

"And why is that?"

"Because..." My voice trailed off. I couldn't think of anything. "Because it's my life, and I need to figure out how it's all going to work."

"I agree, but that doesn't mean you have to do it all yourself."

"I know. It's just all confusing." That was the understatement of the year. I honestly didn't know if I resisted reaching out because a part of me wanted to prove that I was better at raising a child than my mother had been when she had me. Or was it because I needed to prove to myself that I was a strong and capable person? I also feared being a burden to my friends. Perhaps I was simply avoiding Alex? Maybe, it was all of the above.

We reached the park, ending our conversation as Noah took off, running toward the swings. Lucy, I was happy to see, was right on his heels.

Since the park was empty, I tied Gunner to the slide so he could watch us but not get hit by a swing.

I followed Alex's lead at the park and pushed Lucy. Each step I took increased my growing disconnect with him. I didn't want to hurt him, but he was too big a distraction. The night we spent together, he'd asked me to tell him if I was hung up on Daniel. At the time, I said no and meant it. But in the wake of my mother's death, I was no longer certain. And I owed it to Alex not to lead him on.

Besides, I had no time for a relationship. Lucy needed all my attention. In a few short weeks, she'd lost her mother and moved in with a stranger. I had to make this work and ensure Lucy knew how loved and wanted she was.

When the kids were done swinging, we helped them out, and Lucy followed Noah to an undisturbed patch of snow. They both dropped to the ground and made snow angels, and Alex pulled buckets and shovels from his backpack and passed them to the kids.

"You're prepared," I said, sitting on a bench.

"You have to be ready for anything," Alex said.

"I guess I have a lot to learn."

"You'll figure it out."

And there was my opening. "I know, and I have to make that my priority. That's why I think it's best if we don't pursue anything romantic right now."

"Oh." He leaned forward, resting his elbows on his knees and gazing across the park. His head dropped briefly, then he sat back up and met my eyes. His face, normally so expressive, was utterly stoic. "You're right. That makes complete sense."

That was the response I wanted. So why did I feel like I'd been punched in the gut?

The uneasy silence between us was suddenly broken by a piercing wail. Noah had scooped up snow and was dumping it over Lucy's head.

"Noah," Alex yelled as we both ran toward them. But when we reached them, both Lucy and Noah were laughing.

"Snowstorm," said Noah.

"Snowstorm," echoed Lucy, who began filling her bucket with snow.

Noah sat down. "My turn."

"Actually, I think it's time to go," Alex said. "Pass me the buckets, please. Noah, you can be first next time."

"No, Daddy, no," Noah whined.

"Sorry, buddy."

"No fair," said Noah.

"No fair," repeated Lucy.

"How about this?" I suggested. "On the way home, you can take turns holding Gunner's leash."

"Me first," said Lucy.

"No, me," said Noah.

They both ran to Gunner, who was jumping up and down from all the excitement.

"See, you got the hang of this already," Alex said, although his voice was noticeably flat.

I forced a smile, but the comfortable playfulness between us was gone.

After dinner, I gave Lucy a bath. I filled the bathtub with warm water and added some bubbles, smiling as my sister squealed with delight. Finally, she was smiling more. In fact, she smiled more that day than all of our time together combined.

More energetic than her previous times in the bath, she began splashing around, sending soap and water flying in every direction. As I started wiping up the floor, Lucy squealed even louder, and I looked up to see Gunner heaving his body over the side of the tub. Water splashed over the edge like a tidal wave, leaving me drenched. Not that Gunner or Lucy noticed. They were busy playing with a toy boat that Lucy kept dipping underwater as Gunner tried to bite it, making her laugh uncontrollably.

As I dried myself off with one of the few remaining towels, I couldn't help but smile at my sister's infectious joy. It reminded me of the first bath I'd given Gunner, and that relationship had turned out better than anything I could have imagined.

Maybe we were on the right track.

# 20

My head dropped, and I quickly jerked it back up while having dinner with Lucy. *Did I seriously doze off while eating?*

I'd survived my first day back at work, and holy moly, what a day. No matter how much I had prepared the night before, the morning turned out to be utter chaos. Jenna had offered to drop Lucy off at daycare to give me more time, but I wanted to be the one to do it as it was her first day.

I checked the clock and saw it was only seven, but as soon as I got Lucy to bed, I planned to go straight to sleep myself.

As I was washing the dishes, we heard tapping on the front window. Gunner raced to the window, and I joined him. Together, we peeked outside to see Alex and Noah. I went to the door and let them in, wondering what Alex wanted. His face had been so deadpan after our talk yesterday that I assumed it would be a long time before we saw one another again.

"Hey," he said, "Noah and I were baking some bread, so we thought we'd bring you a loaf."

"You baked us bread?"

"We did," he said, handing me a still-warm loaf wrapped in a tea towel. "Consider it a friendship offering. I wanted to—"

Noah ran past us and darted into my apartment. Lucy was holding up a book, and Noah was scrambling to sit beside her on the futon.

"That's one of Noah's favorite books," Alex explained.

"Yeah. Lucy likes that one, too."

Alex nodded. "Anyway, as I was saying, I thought about what you said at the park, and even though it stung, I get it. Lucy has to be your priority, just as Noah is mine. And this whole situation is new for you. So, friends, it is. I only hope you don't completely shut the door on something potentially in the future."

He was so sweet and sincere that I couldn't say no. Instead, I left my answer vague. "Thank you. And who knows what the future holds?"

After a long pause, he spoke again. "Can I read them the book to give you a little break?"

"Do I look that frazzled?"

He gave me a lopsided grin. "It's understandable, considering it's your first day back at work."

My immediate reaction was to insist I was fine, but that was surpassed by my desire to finish everything for the next day so I could get to bed. Plus, he'd baked us bread; if that didn't soften your resolve, nothing would. "Thanks. I do need to make our lunches for tomorrow after I finish the dishes."

"Okay then, now's your chance."

Alex sat between Noah and Lucy on the futon while I finished the dishes and made our lunches. Warmth blossomed through my heart as I heard Alex reading to the two kids. This sweet domestic scene had me feeling like I'd stepped inside a storybook. In my less-than-ideal childhood, I had always dreamed of having moments like this, and now it was happening, not for me, but for Lucy.

But the magic didn't last long. "Uh oh," cried Lucy, who slid off the futon and ran for the bathroom, panicking.

Beside Alex was a wet spot.

"Oh dear," I said, quickly following Lucy, only to find the door locked. "Lucy, open the door, please."

"Me clean," she said.

"Let me help you," I offered, trying to remain calm.

"I do it."

Before I could argue, the bath faucet turned on. My mind raced with worry as I stared at the locked door. The knob had no keyhole or any way to unlock it from the outside.

"Need a hand?"

I jumped at Alex's voice. "I don't know what to do. I've never locked this door before. When it's just me, which is pretty much all the time, I don't even bother closing it."

"I can get my toolbox."

"No. Well, not yet anyway. Let's try getting her to open it first." My chest tightened at all the potential dangers in the bathroom, but I tried to keep my voice as steady as possible. "Lucy, I need you to open the door, please."

"Not finished."

Gunner sat at my feet and tapped his paw against the door. That's when an idea struck me. "Hey Lucy, Gunner's here, and he's tapping on the door. I think he wants a bath, too."

"Okay," she said, and the doorknob rattled. "Can't do it."

I glanced at Alex, who squeezed my shoulder reassuringly as if saying, "You got this."

Closing my eyes, I tried to recall the lock mechanism. "Okay. Under the doorknob, there's a small lever. Try moving it to the other side." We heard more rattling, then finally a click, and the latch released. With a sigh of relief, I turned the knob and opened the door to find Lucy stepping into the bath.

"Come, Gunny," Lucy said, beckoning Gunner. He entered the bathroom, sniffed Lucy's pile of clothes on the floor, then stuck his head over the tub's edge and began drinking, making Lucy and Noah laugh.

"I'm glad Lucy is okay, but we should probably get out of your way. You know what they say about too many cooks in the kitchen. There must be a saying like that for bathrooms."

"I don't know about that, but yeah, I should take care of this. Thanks for the bread," I said. "And, you know, for understanding."

Alex maintained eye contact with me for several quiet moments, revealing such compassionate understanding that it reached into the depths of my soul, and I felt I didn't deserve such a friend. Then he broke our gaze and said, "No worries. Come on, Noah." He picked up his son and held him in his arms. "We'll let ourselves out."

I knew I would think about Alex's look as I drifted off to sleep, but for now, my attention returned to Lucy's chaotic world.

I checked the temperature of the bathwater before sitting on the radiator, watching it fill up, and enjoying the sound of Lucy's laughter as Gunner tried to bite a plastic boat that floated by.

Lucy's clothes needed to be laundered, but that could wait until tomorrow. In the meantime, I rinsed out her underwear and hung them to dry.

Just as I thought things were going well, Lucy suddenly yelled, "Poo!" My head snapped toward the tub, where a small poop bobbed below the surface of the water. Gunner leaned forward, his mouth open.

"Ew! No. Stop." I reached into the tub and retrieved the turd. Disgusted, I dropped it into the toilet and scrubbed my hands clean. As exhaustion washed over me, I lifted Lucy out of the tub, soaped up a washcloth, and wiped her down. So much for that early night.

With Lucy finally clean and dry, I emerged from the bathroom, leaving her to put her pajamas on as she insisted. My heart nearly stopped when

I found Stephanie sitting on the couch. I decided not to mention the wet spot.

"Hey," she stood and wrapped me in a hug. "Sorry to surprise you. I saw Alex and Noah, so I figured you were still up, but I would have come in regardless. How could I not after reading your email? I can't believe you have a sister. You had better start talking because you should have called me. I don't care that I was on my honeymoon. This is big news. Oh, and there was a wet spot on the couch. I kind of guessed what it was and cleaned it for you."

"Thank you. It's been a bit chaotic," I said as tears began to fall.

She hugged me tighter, then pulled away, holding my shoulders and staring at me squarely. "We're here for you. You know that, right?"

I nodded, wiping my eyes. "I'm sorry. It's been a bit overwhelming, that's all."

"Of course it is. Your life has been turned upside down."

"How about you tell me about your honeymoon?"

"My honeymoon," she began, "was absolutely wonderful, but that's for another time." She released my shoulders, filled the kettle with water, and found my selection of tea. I pointed to the one I wanted. Having a friend who knew exactly what I needed was so lovely.

"I would have come over earlier, but we had to pick up a few things first. Jake should be here any minute now."

"It's great to have you both back, but I have to get Lucy to bed."

"I know, but trust me. This will help."

I raised an eyebrow.

"So, how about you introduce us?" Stephanie asked, tilting her head toward the bathroom.

Lucy stood behind me in her footed pajamas, but before I could introduce them, Stephanie whispered, "Oh my gosh," and squatted down to face my sister. "You must be Lucy," she said. "I'm Stephanie, your sister's best friend, and I'm so glad to meet you."

Lucy popped her thumb in her mouth and wrapped an arm around my leg. My heart nearly melted with love as my sister sought reassurance from me. Me!

"Hello, hello," Jake's voice called out from the hall.

"Oh, goodie," Stephanie said, jumping up. She opened the door and let him in.

"Hey, Vic," Jake said, leaning in and kissing me on the cheek. In his arms was a tiny bed.

"It's a toddler bed," Stephanie said excitedly. "I'm certain it will fit under the window. It might be a tight fit, but at least it's her own space."

I watched, speechless, as Stephanie cleared a spot and Jake placed the bed down. "Be right back," he said.

Stephanie moved the bed into position, and Jake returned with the mattress and a large bag.

"It fits a crib mattress, so it's nice and small," said Stephanie.

Jake laid the mattress down while Stephanie opened the bag and made the bed. "Okay, I may have had some fun with this," she admitted as pink bedding was removed from the bag.

The sheets were pale pink, while the comforter was the color of bubblegum and printed with cartoon dogs and cats. There was also a giant stuffed dog, a smaller stuffed cat, and a big fluffy pillow.

"Ta-da," Stephanie sang when she finished. "What do you think, Lucy? This is for you."

Lucy turned to me, her eyes wide with shock. A lump the size of Kansas formed in my throat when I realized she was waiting for my approval.

I nodded. "Go on. Try it out."

My sister squealed with delight, grabbed Bluey, and then jumped onto her new bed. She hugged all the new stuffed animals, then crawled under the sheets like she was burrowing in for winter. The next thing we knew, Gunner joined in, and soon, the two of them were cuddled up under the covers.

"I'm going to assume she likes it," Jake said, grinning.

"I don't know what to say," I finally managed. "Thank you both so much. This is so incredibly thoughtful."

"Anything for you, Vic. And I know it's cramped, but it's just until you get a bigger place. I'm assuming you will, right?" asked Stephanie.

I nodded, suddenly feeling like the air had been sucked out of my lungs. If things worked out with Lucy—and they had to—then yes, moving would be necessary. But how could I?

I'd be leaving the first real home I'd ever had.

But it wasn't only that. What if Daniel came by?

# 21

As the days passed, Lucy and I settled into a comfortable routine, our relationship strengthening as we learned more about each other. Despite this, I couldn't deny the longing for a break, so when Jenna invited Lucy for dinner and a playdate, I eagerly accepted.

Those few hours away would allow me to escape and recharge. Instead of taking a relaxing bath or indulging in a much-needed nap, I chose to lose myself in the vibrant colors and details of painting.

Surprisingly, while I needed to create, I wasn't back to using art as an outlet for my deepest, darkest thoughts. Despite all the recent changes and challenges in my life, I found peace and contentment in my role as a big sister and in my mother's unexpected attempt to reconnect with me. Perhaps, finally, healing was within reach.

I had been creating a mural at the animal shelter for a few months, and it was that project I worked on. When I initially mentioned this project to Oliver, he thought it was a waste of my talent and viewed it as very pedestrian. But I didn't see it that way. This was a tribute and a thank you to the place that had changed the trajectory of my life. I still found it hard to believe that I started volunteering there to simply beef up my resume. Instead, I made friends and found a community. It was there that I became friends with Mariam, Daniel's mother. Suppose Mariam had never invited me to Thanksgiving dinner, and Daniel and I never started chatting. What would have become of my life?

Stepping back, I examined the mural in front of me. It was a delicate balance to capture both humor and emotion. I decided to create a class photo page, as if from a yearbook, featuring real adopted dogs and cats. Under each image, I had written a brief description. For Gunner, I wrote: 'Gunner. Class of 2000. Rescued from an abandoned house, he now loves belly rubs and jogging. Voted most likely to sneak a lick from your ice cream cone.'

I have no idea where the inspiration came from. Unlike my peers, I never bought a high school yearbook. Nor did we have any school pictures, even from elementary school. School was a nightmare that had to be endured. Why would I want to be reminded of the bullies who made my life miserable? As for my mother, her focus was always her next fix, not capturing memories in photos.

But things were different for Lucy. She already had a better start than I did, and I was determined to give her everything I never had, including attention. That's why working on the mural was bittersweet. As soon as it was finished, I would stop volunteering.

The shelter was closed for the day, leaving a skeleton crew behind to care for the animals overnight, so I was surprised to hear footsteps in the main corridor. I turned to see Francois, the volunteer coordinator and Darcy's significant other, walking toward me with a plastic container.

"Thanks again for the cookies. They were great," he said, handing me the empty container. "At least the lonely one I ate. Darcy snarfed down the rest. She was like an angry bear if I put my hand anywhere near them. Don't tell her I said that. I want to live to see the birth of our child."

"Your secret is safe with me," I said.

He stood back, taking in the mural. "I can't believe you're almost done. It's amazing," he said. "We're so lucky to benefit from your talent.

From the sketch of the place in the office to the mural to the drawings you do for fundraising, we really lucked out when you walked through our door."

"Thanks. This place is important to me."

"And I can't wait to meet your sister," Francois continued. "Abby was telling me all about her when she and Jenna came by the other day. Well, have a good night," Francois said. "It's my turn to make dinner, and I don't want to keep Darcy waiting."

As soon as he was gone, I let my body slide down the wall until I was sitting on the cold linoleum floor. Why hadn't I found the courage to tell Francois I was quitting? The thought had been on my mind for weeks, yet when the perfect opportunity arose, I couldn't bring myself to do it.

His words echoed in my mind, reminding me of all the activities and projects I had been involved in at the shelter—how could I abandon it now? Since moving to Montreal, the shelter has been my one constant source of stability and purpose. Despite everything else weighing on my mind, I knew deep down that I wasn't ready to give that up yet.

Besides, Abby accompanied Jenna when she volunteered. Maybe I could bring Lucy?

But Jenna started volunteering to improve her grooming skills so that she would find a better job and give Abby a better life. I would be doing it for myself. Did that make me selfish, like my mother?

As my thoughts spiraled downward, I dipped my brush into the paint and continued on. All I could do, for now, was finish the mural.

22

As THE DOOR TO the art shop swung open, a gust of frosty November air rushed in behind us. Gunner passed by Isabelle, giving her a quick sniff. Then, he walked into the office and plopped down beside Celine, sighing with exhaustion as if he'd just run a marathon. I couldn't help but envy him for his nap.

"How's it going?" Isabelle asked with a smile, but something about her expression seemed off, almost like a mask hiding something deeper. My stomach knotted at the sight of it.

"We're surviving."

"Are you going to bring Lucy by so I can meet her one day?"

"Yeah, I can do that."

Isabelle nodded, then ran a hand through her hair and sighed. "Good, but it had better be soon."

The knot in my stomach tightened. "What do you mean? That doesn't sound good," I said, knowing it must have to do with the sale of the store.

"It's not. But it's not monumentally bad, either. It depends."

I hung up my coat and slipped my apron on, trying to keep myself calm before walking over to Isabelle. "Tell me."

She took a deep breath. "I've handed in my two-week notice."

I gasped, my hand flying to cover my mouth in shock. "What? Why? Because Mr. Henderson sold the store?"

Isabelle nodded.

"But that doesn't mean you have to quit. This place can't run without you. And we'd miss you so much."

She shrugged nonchalantly, but her resignation was apparent. "The new company is a large chain and will send its own manager here. They offered me the role of assistant manager, but I don't want to be second in command. I turned this store around. A demotion on top of having someone new tell me what to do would be too infuriating. I can't do it."

My mind went blank as I tried to process the news. This store had been my sanctuary, and Isabelle was a crucial part of that. The thought of her leaving sent a painful jolt through me. Despite knowing the store's sale loomed in the future, it still felt like a gut-wrenching shock. My heart clenched at the idea of someone else taking over, disrupting the comfortable atmosphere that Isabelle had created. From the day Isabelle hired me full-time, this store was a part of my life. Moving forward, it would be nothing more than a job.

The last few weeks had brought about so much change; it was as if I stood in the eye of a tornado while every aspect of my life was shaken about, including the art store. I glanced at the familiar shelves and displays, feeling betrayed. Et tu, Brutis?

Isabelle's words cut through my thoughts. "I don't know what your plans are, what with your cake business with Alex, but I recommended you for the assistant manager position. It would mean more money, which would help now that you have Lucy, but I doubt they'll keep the pet-friendly policy. None of their other stores do, and I think, based on the location, this one is slated to become the flagship store."

"That was kind of you, thanks. When does the new manager start?"

"One week from now," Isabelle replied solemnly.

"One week? Wow. So what are you going to do?" I asked her, not wanting to focus solely on my problems. Isabelle was losing a lot more than I was with the store's sale.

"I'll probably help with my dad's business while I figure out my next step. I think I might be ready for a change. The idea of going out west is appealing. It's something I've wanted to do for a while now. Maybe this is the push I need to take that leap."

I couldn't fathom why anyone would want to leave the supportive family and close group of friends that Isabelle had, but then again, maybe that's what gave her the confidence and courage to make such a big change. In a burst of emotion, I stepped forward and pulled her into a hug. "We'll miss you. It won't be the same without you."

"I'll miss you too, and I know Celine will miss Gunner," she said, wiping a tear off her cheek. "But you know what they say, the only constant is change."

I gave her a wry smile. Considering all the changes my life had undergone recently, I couldn't help but think the phrase 'too much of a good thing' applied to my situation.

⊷⊶ ⋅+⋅ ⊷⊶

After an emotionally grueling day at work, I returned home to find a message from Alex waiting for me on my answering machine.

"I made some pizza and thought you and Lucy might want to join us for dinner and a movie." The thought of seeing him, having him wrap his arms around me and hold me close while I expressed my distress over the art store sale, was almost overpowering. His calm demeanor and reassuring smile would cheer me up, but something held me back. I sank onto the couch, feeling a mix of guilt and longing wash over me. I hadn't spoken to Alex since he'd come by with the freshly baked bread, and his message only reminded me of the growing distance between us.

Which was all on me. Alex was attempting to connect, whereas I was avoiding him.

There was no time to dwell on it because I heard laughter coming from Jenna's apartment, reminding me to collect Lucy. Having Jenna pick her up from daycare tonight had been a lifesaver.

"Knock, knock," I said, entering her apartment. Jenna stood in the kitchen, stirring something on the stove.

"Oh, hey," Jenna said. "Matt's out for the evening. Want to join me and Abby for dinner? Girls' night in?"

I contemplated Alex's message. If I stayed at Jenna's, there would be no pressure to reply. When I eventually saw him again, I could simply explain that I was at Jenna's place. Lucy was having fun, so why pull her away from that? "Yeah, that sounds amazing. Can I do anything?"

"Nope. Have a seat and kick your feet up. Tell me how it's going?"

"Where to begin?" I said as I collapsed onto a chair.

"That bad, huh?"

Tears formed, and Jenna noticed before I could look away.

"Vic, what is it?"

"It's my job. The store sale has gone through, and the new owners are bringing in their own manager."I took a deep breath. "Isabelle quit."

"Oh no, I'm sorry to hear that."

"The only good thing is that Isabelle recommended me for the assistant manager position. It will be a pay raise, but I won't be able to take Gunner anymore, and Isabelle and I were always accommodating over each other's schedules. Things will be a lot more rigid. And not nearly as much fun."

"You don't know that for sure."

"It's a good guess."

"Will you still have your cake side hustle with Alex?"

"I'm putting that on the back burner."

"Why? I thought you wanted the money."

"I do, but I also need time to focus on Lucy. Besides, I told Alex I only wanted to be friends. Now that we've been intimate, working together would be weird."

"I thought you liked him."

"I do. A lot," I admitted, "But sometimes timing is everything, and now is not a good time."

Jenna stopped stirring the pasta and sat down beside me. "I completely understand that you need time to adjust to having Lucy, but you still have to live your life. Maybe take it slow instead of stopping it all together."

"He agreed we could be friends for the time being, but he's too big of a distraction. I grew up with a mother who didn't have the time of day for me. I don't want to make that mistake with Lucy."

"You won't."

"How do you know?"

"Because you're a loving, caring person. And if Alex makes you happy, you should—"

"Momma," Abby yelled. "We need you."

Jenna sighed, wiping her hands on a tea towel. "Can you stir the sauce for me while I find out what's going on?"

"Sure," I said, standing and moving toward the stove. As I stirred, the bubbling sauce filled the kitchen with its rich aroma, a stark contrast to the turmoil in my mind. I thought back to my conversation with Isabelle earlier, how her resignation had forced me to confront another impending change in my life. Isabelle would miss the store as she'd worked there for five years, but she couldn't hide her excitement over the new chapter in her life. Already, she'd spent the afternoon researching interesting towns out west. She was ready to seek new experiences, whereas I wanted the opposite.

"Lucy had an accident. I got her changed into Abby's old pajamas, and her clothes are in a bag by the door," Jenna said, walking into the kitchen.

"That's her third accident. I don't know why she keeps doing that. Do you think something's wrong? Should I take her to a doctor?"

"I shouldn't think so. Kids that age have accidents. She's still so young, and there's been a lot of change."

"I guess. Gunner peed in my apartment a few times when I got him."

"It's pretty much the same thing, now about Alex..."

"Let's talk about him another time. I'm still reeling from the news of Isabelle quitting and the sale of the store. I don't have enough gray matter to process my feelings for Alex right now. Besides," I put the wooden spoon down, "I think the sauce is ready."

"Okay. I'll get the girls to wash their hands. But first..." Jenna wrapped me in a hug. "I love you. You know that, right?"

"I know. I love you too, and thanks."

"And that dog grooming job is still on the table if you want it. It won't be until the new year and will only be part-time, but it's yours if you need it."

"I appreciate that. Now, while you take the kids to wash their hands, I'm going to throw Lucy's clothes in the sink to soak. I'll be right back."

I grabbed the bag of laundry and raced down to my apartment. On the way to the bathroom, I noticed my answering machine was blinking with a new message. *Alex?*

In the bathroom, I filled the sink with water and submerged Lucy's soiled clothing. On my way back to Jenna's, I couldn't resist pressing the play button on the answering machine, and the familiar sound of Alex's voice filled the room. "Sorry we missed you. We'll have to do pizza and a movie another day. Call me when you can. I just want to know how you're doing."

It wasn't until I reached the landing in front of Jenna's place that it hit me—for the first time since Daniel left, his name hadn't been the first thing on my mind when I saw the flashing light on my answering machine.

Now that was a change of monumental proportion.

# 23

As the sun peeked through the windows on Sunday morning, I found myself coping with my stress through frenzied cleaning. I handed Lucy a cloth, and she eagerly joined in, her tiny hand gripping it tightly and moving in circular motions against the cupboard doors. But before I had finished vacuuming, she'd moved on to wiping Gunner, who playfully tugged on the cloth with his teeth, and before I knew it, they were engaged in a game of tug of war.

Once the kitchen and bathroom were scrubbed to a shine, Lucy and I stripped her bed so I could wash her sheets. As I gathered mine together, I removed the photograph of Daniel and me from my pillowcase, its edges softened and frayed. I gently trace my fingers over the image, remembering how his arm felt around my waist, the sound of his laughter, and how his kisses tasted of love as bright and hot as the sunshine. Then, a few days later, he left my life forever. Forever.

"I don't know what I'm doing anymore," I said to his image, then placed the photo on the table.

Bundling up my bedding, I called to Lucy, "Grab your sheets. We'll take them to the washer." We headed to the basement and placed our washing in the machine. On our way back up, we heard knocking at the front door and found Gunner sitting there, his tail wagging.

I opened it to find Alex on the doorstep. He was wearing a navy wool fisherman sweater and old, worn jeans. The sweater hugged his broad shoulders and emphasized the muscles in his arms, and his jeans were faded in all the right places. My heart skipped a beat at the sight of him, a smile forming on his lips as he held a small white box in his arms.

"Hey," he said. "Can I come in?"

"Of course," I said, stepping back. "But we might put you to work. Lucy and I are deep cleaning today."

"How about I provide the snacks? We've started our Christmas baking at work, so I thought I'd bring you a selection of treats. I remember you saying that one of your friends likes the bakery, so I brought enough to share."

His rugged features and kind smile reminded me of how good it felt to be in his arms, and I yearned to do that now, to feel his warm body through the soft wool of his sweater, to listen to his heartbeat, and to hold him close. But I remained frozen, unable to move or touch him, my heart fluttering like a flock of birds in my chest. The weight of indecision dragged me down like a net being pulled through the ocean. It was exhausting, and I was tired of it taking up so much emotional energy when I already had so much to deal with.

"Wow. That's super thoughtful of you, thanks. I'll make sure Matt gets some, but I better get back to work now."

"Hang on. I have the feeling you're avoiding me. Have I done something to upset you?" he asked.

I hesitated, unsure how to answer. How could I explain the complex emotions that were swirling inside me? I couldn't. Instead, I said, "No. Of course not. It's that...Lucy is my main focus right now."

"I completely understand. You have a lot to deal with. I'm not trying to pressure you. Taking things slowly right now makes sense."

His understanding made this even more difficult.

"I guess," he began, then took a deep breath, "I guess I'm trying to figure out where, and if, I fit in."

"Can we talk later, please?" I glanced at Lucy, not wanting her to hear our conversation.

"Sure, I'm just worried another week will go by."

"What about tonight? Maybe we can take the kids to the park before dinner. We can talk while they play." Not that I knew what I'd say.

"Noah's with his mom this weekend. I'm picking him up later, and then we're having dinner with my parents."

"Oh, okay. Well, soon then."

An uncomfortable silence filled the room. Then I noticed his gaze locked on the picture of Daniel and me sitting on the table. His demeanor changed, and I could almost see his heart break in front of me. "Can you be honest with me, please?" he asked.

"Of course."

"This guy from your past, you're not over him, are you?"

How could I answer him honestly when I wasn't sure myself? My emotions were too tangled and conflicted. How could I explain that I felt guilty for thinking of Daniel when I was with him but felt like I'd cheated on Daniel when I longed to be with Alex? Especially since Daniel had been gone for over a year. It didn't make sense, even to me. "It's complicated," I finally confessed, knowing the answer was vague but unsure how else to explain it.

My words hung in the air like a fog. I shifted uncomfortably and fiddled with the hem of my shirt.

"I guess that's not the answer I was hoping for," he finally said, his eyes full of disappointment. "You know, I wasn't looking to date anyone, but we connected. Working with you was great. Things just clicked, both professionally and personally. I couldn't help but be drawn to you, and I thought you felt the same way. But aside from the night of Stephanie's wedding, you've been holding back. And this is why, isn't it?" He tapped the picture with a finger. "You said he's in the past, but here he is. I can't compete with a ghost, Vic. Like I said before," Alex continued, his voice cracking slightly, "I don't mind taking things slow. In fact, I think it's a good idea, especially as there are kids involved, but I at least need to know that we're on the same page. The problem is, only part of you is with me. Most of you is still with him."

I couldn't answer.

"I knew it." His long blink and helpless head shake conveyed his disappointment more than any words could.

"I'm sorry," I said, reaching out to touch his arm in a feeble attempt at comfort.

"Don't." He pulled away, taking a deep breath as if trying to contain his emotions. "I'm sorry, too. I think we could have had something amazing. And this isn't about the cake business. We had the potential to build something great together, including Lucy and Noah. But I guess I was wrong. Take care of yourself, Vicki." And with that, he walked out.

I didn't attempt to stop him.

Maybe I'd become accustomed to watching the people I care about leave me.

"No cry," Lucy said, tapping my leg.

I gently brushed the tears from my cheeks with the back of my hand, then kneeled down to lift her into my arms. As I nestled my face against her neck, I breathed in deeply, taking in the sweet scent of baby powder, laundry detergent, and innocence. A warmth spread through my heart as she wrapped her tiny arms around my neck and nuzzled into me, seeking comfort. Despite the pain and tears that had just fallen, this moment with Lucy brought a sense of peace and joy.

"I think we've done enough work for the day, don't you? Want to do some coloring?"

"Okay."

I gave her a big squeeze and sat her at the table. Then I got out the pencil crayons and two coloring books, one for her and one for me. Even though I was coloring a picture of a kitten with a ball of yarn, the soft scratching sound of the pencil crayon against the page was like a soothing lullaby, calming my mind. It was precisely what I needed to do, so we sat together and colored until the washing machine buzzed in the basement.

We ran down and put our sheets into the dryer. Back upstairs, Lucy returned to coloring while I picked up the phone and dialed Stephanie.

"Hey, Steph. Did you want to come over for some tea later?"

"Sure, what's up?"

"I could use your advice."

"You seek my council? Sure. I'll be over in about an hour."

"Thanks so much. See you then."

Stephanie arrived an hour later as Lucy and Gunner were settling into her freshly made bed for a nap. I motioned for her to keep her voice down to avoid disturbing Lucy.

She eyed the treats in my kitchen. "Have you been baking?"

"Alex brought them."

"He did, did he?"

"That's kind of what I wanted to talk to you about."

"Uh-oh. It sounds like you had better make a big pot of tea. I have a feeling this might take a while." She kicked off her boots and tossed her jacket onto the coat tree before heading to the table. Sitting down with perfect posture, she folded her hands in front of her and gave me her undivided attention. "Okay, Dr. Stephanie is ready."

Over a cup of chamomile tea, I told her about my situation at work. But as I spoke, Stephanie challenged my negative assumptions, and I realized that while I didn't like the situation, it wasn't as bad as I'd built it up to be. People changed jobs. That was life. Yes, I would miss Isabelle, but I still had a job and possibly a promotion. If I didn't like it, I could find something new in the future, but with everything else I had going on, it was better to stay where I was and make the best of it.

"That one was easy," Stephanie said. "What's next?"

"This one's a bit more complicated," I said, then proceeded to tell her about my earlier conversation with Alex, my conflicting feelings, and how I kept flip-flopping between Alex and Daniel. "It's like I'm holding a daisy and plucking off the petals like kids do, but instead of 'he loves me, he loves me not,' it's 'I like Alex, but what about Daniel,' over and over and over again."

"It might not be as complicated as you think," Stephanie began.

"How so?"

"Well, you simply have to ask yourself two questions. First question: are you ready to move past Daniel, yes or no? Second question: can you handle a relationship now, yes or no?"

"It's not that easy."

"It is if you want it to be." She reached across the table and grasped my hands. Her touch was gentle and comforting, a stark contrast to the cold reality of her words. "Daniel is long gone. I know that's harsh, but it's true. You have this idealized image of your relationship in your mind, but you were only together for six weeks. Of course, it was perfect; it was shiny and new and exciting. Which was exactly what you needed at that time. But that time is over. You're a different person now, stronger and wiser from your experiences. Don't you want more from love than a memory?"

"Yes, of course I do, but as soon as I think about moving forward with Alex, I panic and turn back to Daniel. It's like I've created a love triangle where one doesn't exist."

Stephanie raised a well-plucked eyebrow, her expression thoughtful as she sipped her tea. "Interesting," she mused. "Okay, so let me ask you this:

were you interested in dating Alex before you found out your mother died and that you had a sister?"

I thought back to the night I'd spent with Alex, the chemistry and the closeness. "Yes."

"So that was a big decision for you, right? Until Alex, you hadn't been with anyone since Daniel. One might argue that dating Alex was a big change for you, and forgive me if I'm wrong, but as far as I know, you're not a big fan of change."

"I don't love it," I agreed.

"Okay, so the moment you make one change, bigger changes are thrust upon you. On top of the emotional aftermath of your mother's passing, you now have a sister to raise. And then there's the store being sold and Isabelle quitting."

"All true, and to be honest with you, it's going to take me some time to process everything. Maybe even therapy."

"Yeah, well, join the club. My point is that with all these changes, maybe it's not that you're hung up on Daniel. It's that you're hung up on having Daniel as a stable part of your life. Not physically, obviously, as he's not here, but by hanging on to the idea of Daniel, you have one part of your life that you can control. Nothing is going to change about Daniel. It's a safe zone."

I rested my head in my hands, the weight of her words heavy on my mind. I'd never thought of it that way, but it all made perfect sense. It explained why I was reluctant to quit volunteering at the animal shelter, why I overreacted at Isabelle's resignation, and why I avoided Alex. I wanted some of the stability that existed in my life prior to the unexpected call from Walter DiAngelo that turned everything upside down. "So what do I do?"

"Well, before you do anything, you need to answer my second question: do you want a relationship now? If yes, talk to Alex. If not, move on and keep going. Easy peasy." Stephanie stretched and checked the time. "I'm sorry to say this, but I have to go soon. Before I do, however, I might have time to solve world hunger."

"Ha, ha. But seriously, thanks. You've given me a lot to think about."

"That's why they pay me the big bucks." She got up, slipped on her coat and boots, and hugged me. "Seriously, you're good?"

"Yeah. I think I am."

"Then my work here is done."

As she left my apartment, she swung open the front door and almost tripped over a bouquet of flowers sitting on the doorstep. "Well, well, well, what do we have here?" She plucked the card from the bouquet and read, "For Vicki."

Steph passed me the flowers with a mischievous glint in her eye. "I wonder who these could be from?"

"I don't know," I said, but my heart whispered please be from Alex. As soon as that thought popped into my head, I knew I had my feelings sorted out. I wanted them to be from Alex. Not Daniel.

"Read the card and find out. And do it out loud. I'm deeply invested now."

With trembling hands, I opened the envelope and unfolded the card. "Even though it didn't work out, I'm glad to have met you and hope you find the happiness you deserve. Alex."

"Oh my God, that was so sweet. Are you okay?" Stephanie asked.

I nodded, too full of emotion to speak. This was Alex's way of saying goodbye. The bouquet suddenly felt heavier, the delicate petals and stems remaining strong and beautiful despite the crushing weight of what could have been.

# 24

I'd spent Sunday night lying awake, thinking of Alex. But, thanks to my conversation with Stephanie, I arrived at work on Monday feeling more settled than I had been in a long time. Reminding myself of Isabelle's words that change is the only constant, I was determined to embrace whatever came next, maybe not with open arms, but I would accept it and do my best to succeed. Good thing, too, because as I opened the laptop and checked my inbox, I was greeted by an official email from Mr. Henderson. It detailed Isabelle's departure and introduced our new manager, setting the stage for a period of transition.

Attached to the email were several posters announcing the new ownership. I was to print them off and hang them in select locations. I wasn't sure how all our customers would react. The majority would remain indifferent so long as we still stocked what they required, but I supposed a select few would view the shift toward corporate ownership with skepticism. But I doubted it would hurt the bottom line as there weren't a lot of art shops around, especially in such a prime downtown location. That meant my job would be safe for the near future, giving me time to consider different options. Or, who knew? Maybe I'd love it under the new company banner.

With my change in attitude, the quiet Monday morning passed pleasantly. Isabelle breezed in at noon with coffee and donuts, our Monday tradition, and we reviewed the schedule for the week.

"So, we need to start looking for temporary Christmas help, and this year, I'm going to ask you to do the interviews and hiring."

"Me?" I choked out, my mouth full of coffee.

"Yes. It's time for you to take on additional responsibilities. Besides, you've done that job. You should know exactly the kind of person the store needs."

*Personal growth, personal growth*, I chanted to myself. "You're right, I do. Thanks." I'd post a sign in the store window by the end of the day. We had enough art students looking for work that I wouldn't need to post an ad elsewhere. That's how I found the job two years ago, and now, I'm doing the hiring. If only I could tell...Alex. I wanted to share this with Alex. After two years of whispering my news from the top of Mount Royal to a person who'd never reply, I was done. That thought was both liberating and terrifying.

The door jingled, signaling an end to our meeting and pulling me out of my thoughts. I strode out of the office to greet the customer, surprised to find Oliver leaning against the counter. We hadn't seen him since the art show.

"Oliver, how nice to see you." I walked around the counter and gave him a friendly hug. "How is everything going?"

"Wonderful, absolutely wonderful. It's like a dream come true." Oliver's infectious smile lit up his face. This was such a completely different demeanor to his serious, brooding artist persona that I might not have recognized him or assumed this was his brother, save for his clothes, paint-covered jeans, and a sweatshirt that must double as a rag.

"You must be painting again," I reasoned.

"I am," he replied, giddy with excitement. "I'm starting a winter series. Using the impasto technique in oil, I'm focusing on whites and light grays. What size linen canvases do you have? I've been experimenting on wooden panels and want to compare them to canvas."

"Sure. Come with me. I'll show you what we have."

Practically vibrating with energy, he turned to follow me, then stopped. "What's this?" He pointed at the sign beside the cash register.

"Well, the art store's been sold to a larger company," I told him.

"Oh no," he said, his brows furrowing in concern. "Please tell me the store is not closing."

"No. Just new ownership."

"And you two will still be here?"

"Vicki will be," Isabelle said as she walked out of the office and tucked the laptop under the counter. "It's time for me to move on."

"That's a shame. Isabelle, you will be truly missed," Oliver said.

"Thank you," she replied. "And as your career takes off, I can say I knew Oliver Smith when he was an unknown artist."

With a blushing Oliver beside me, we made our way to the back of the shop, stopping in front of the racks of canvases. "The ones you want are in this section here. We only keep the most popular sizes, so if you need something uncommon, call ahead, and I'll order it for you."

"Thanks, Vicki," he said, picking up one of our smaller sizes. "How is your work coming along? Is there anything I can see?"

"Um, well, no. I've been too busy recently," I stammered.

"Don't let her tell you that, Oliver. She's been creating in another medium," Isabelle yelled from across the store.

"You have?" Oliver's interest was piqued. "What have you been working with?"

"I, uh, well..."

"Cake. She's been working with cake," Isabelle said.

"How unusual," Oliver remarked.

"It's not what you think. They were wedding cakes," I said quickly.

"They were works of art," Isabelle continued. "She's downplaying how truly awesome they were."

Oliver's interest only grew, surprising me. "Can I see them?"

"I have pictures in the back," Isabelle said. "She brought them in to show me."

"Wonderful," Oliver said and strode to the front desk, two canvases tucked under his arm. Isabelle produced the pictures, and Oliver studied them with such intensity that it was as if they were potential forgeries he was scrutinizing for authenticity.

"These are spectacular," he said. "I think you've found your calling."

"It's not art. It's cake," I said.

"Yes, but these are unique one-of-a-kind commissions, worthy of the title 'work of art.' I'll be the first to admit that I can be a bit of an art snob, you know that about me, but there's something about these that express both playful joy and deep meaning." He laughed. "That doesn't sound like me, does it? Perhaps it's because I'm in love and seeing the world through a new lens."

"In love?" I had assumed this cheery-faced Oliver was a product of his art exhibit.

Oliver's smile was so broad his eyes crinkled in the corners. "What can I say? I have fallen for the beautiful Celeste Deborough, and she for me. In fact—" he paused, lost in thought as he paced back and forth on the creaky old floorboards. Finally, he continued. "In fact, Celeste is turning thirty on December nineteenth, and we're planning a grand celebration. It will be a black-tie event with a Roaring Twenties theme. Her parents are hiring the caterers, but I'm going to insist that they hire you to make the cake. What do you say?"

Whoa. I was not expecting that. "Um, I don't know. Those cakes were for my best friend. It's nothing I do professionally."

"Yes, but your partner does," Isabelle said.

I shook my head, still uncertain. After how things had ended the other day, I couldn't just approach Alex and say, 'Want to bake a cake?' "I'll have to check with him first. The holiday season is a busy time at the bakery where he works."

"Come on, Vic. Do you honestly think he'd turn down making a cake for Celeste Deborough? It would be all over the society pages. This could launch his business," Isabelle argued.

Both Isabelle and Oliver stared at me with hopeful eyes.

"Okay, fine," I relented, sighing. I'll talk to Alex tonight and let you know soon."

Oliver beamed and leaned in to give me a grateful kiss on the cheek before paying for his supplies and leaving the store.

I glanced across the counter at Isabelle, who smiled innocently at me. "This is too good an opportunity, Vic. You can't let it pass you by."

"I know." And I wouldn't have hesitated if things were normal between Alex and me, but I hadn't yet worked up the courage to talk to him. I planned to admit to him the depths of my feelings. He deserved to know. Whether or not that would persuade him to want to try again, I had no idea. But to start that conversation with 'Hey, want to bake a cake' felt odd and cold. Like maybe I was using him. Still, this wasn't an ordinary cake. Such a high-profile commission would do wonders for his business. I had to secure it for him. It was the least I could do after all he'd done for me.

Isabelle took Celine and Gunner for a mid-afternoon walk while I finished restocking the charcoal. Alone, my mind raced with ideas for a Roaring Twenties cake. A flapper's dress adorned with shimmering tassels, an elegant cocktail cake, or something minimalist, like black silhouettes of iconic twenties images against a crisp white background. There were so many possibilities and the doors this cake could open...if the Deborough family liked it, there's no telling where that would lead. We could be making cakes full-time.

Would Alex and I ever be a *we* again? Alex might refuse to work with me. An apology, even one where I expressed my feelings for him, might not change anything. He told me he had to be careful with his heart. I'd hurt him once. He might not want to risk it again.

# 25

I arrived at Alex's house dressed in jogging gear, Gunner at my side. My heart pounded as if we'd already gone for our run, but we'd yet set out. The warm glow spilling from the windows into the dark evening told me Alex was still up. With a deep breath, I knocked lightly on the door so as not to wake Noah.

Alex answered, his expression cloaked behind a neutral mask the second he saw me.

"Hey," I managed, trying to sound brave and confident. "Can we talk for a minute?"

He hesitated, his fingers absently combing through his hair. I think I aged a year waiting for his response.

"Please?" I added, noting a tinge of desperation had crept into my voice.

Finally, he stepped back, allowing Gunner and me to enter.

"No Lucy?" he asked, speaking for the first time since I'd arrived.

"No. She's in bed. Sylvanna, from the apartment above me, is babysitting. She needed some art supplies for a project, so I said she could come down and use mine. Lucy was already asleep, so it's a good gig for her. And she's often babysitting her nephews, so she knows what to do. Of course, she also cares for Abby because Josh is Abby's father, and I'm sorry. I'm babbling."

A tiny, almost imperceptible smile tugged at the corners of his mouth. "I remember meeting both Sylvanna and Josh at the wedding."

"Yes, of course."

"Why don't we go to the kitchen? That way, we're less likely to wake Noah, and I can get Gunner a bowl of water. I take it you two have been running."

"Actually, we haven't run yet. I wanted to catch you before you went to bed, given how early you start work."

I followed him into the kitchen. All the fun we had baking and icing cakes came flashing back, and I hoped we would make more memories like that. I had to convince him. "About our conversation yesterday," I began. *Wow. Was that only yesterday?* "There are a few things about me you should know."

He placed a bowl of water on the floor for Gunner, giving me a moment to gather my thoughts and muster the courage I would need to get through this. With Daniel, I never hid my true feelings, and because of that, we had an amazing connection. I hoped that would work now.

"I'm listening," he said, eyes fixed on mine with unwavering attention.

"I like you, Alex. A lot. I think about you when I'm at work, as I pick Lucy up from daycare, and when I'm making dinner. But you're right about Daniel. I was holding on to him. The thing is, I was a different person when I met him, someone you might not recognize. But I've grown into the person I am today because of him. Let me explain."

I paused, gathering my thoughts.

"I told you I left home at eighteen because of my mother. What I didn't tell you is that after leaving her, my journey led me to a very toxic relationship that eroded what little self-esteem I already had. Our relationship wasn't violent. Kent hurt me emotionally, and I truly believed I was unworthy of love. We lived together for several years, and even when I decided to leave him, it took me over six months to summon the courage." I helped myself to a glass of water, then continued. "That's when I came to Montreal. A few months later, I met Daniel. Daniel and I had only six weeks together, but during that time, he taught me what real love was. I learned I was both worthy and deserving of love. I grew to like and accept myself. Our time together transformed my life, and I can't ever forget that."

Alex was staring at the floor, but at least he was listening. I continued on.

"Despite knowing we'd gone our separate ways, I clung to his memory, especially when I was worried or sad. Thinking about him was like wrapping myself in a comforting blanket. Daniel was the first person to encourage me, love me, and believe in me. I think part of me was worried that without him, I might go back to the way I was. But Stephanie reminded me that I'm not the person I was when I met him. I'm stronger and more confident, and I have a group of friends to lean on. It's not only that." I took a long sip of water before putting the glass of water down and moving closer to Alex.

"I believed that I had my one shot at love. That there was no one else out there for me. Then I met you, and as we got to know one another and my attraction grew, I found myself ready to explore a relationship. But then Walter DiAngelo called, and amid all the chaos, I panicked. Everything was changing—except Daniel. He remained an immutable beacon, calling to me like a steady heartbeat. And so I clung to it, to him. But in doing so, I pushed you away. Does that make sense?"

Alex's mask had disappeared, and his eyes softened, revealing tenderness and understanding, making me almost weep with relief. "It does. Thank you for sharing that with me."

I moved a bit closer, longing for him to wrap his arms around me. Instead, he walked to the patio doors and stared out at his snowy backyard, his arms crossed. "I know there are no guarantees in life, but if you're holding your relationship with Daniel up on a pedestal, then anything we start will only pale in comparison. I don't want to feel like I'm second best."

"Of course not. I'd never do that to you." My voice grew louder as my emotions soared. "Daniel and I had only six weeks together. It was a beautiful moment in my life. But I want more than six weeks with you. Heck, I've already known you for more than six weeks, and it's not enough. I want to be there to share the good times and the bad. I want to support you, and know that you'll be there for me. I want to make memories and have private jokes. And I know it won't be easy, especially as you have Noah and I have Lucy, but I think the four of us can make a good team."

He ran a hand down his face and turned to me. "You're not the only one with baggage. I could have tried harder to win you over when I felt you were pushing me away, but the harder I fought to keep Simone, the more it hurt when she left, and I didn't want to go through that level of rejection again. So it was easier to let you go."

"But I haven't gone. I'm right here." Feeling a surge of hope, I laced my fingers with his. A spark seemed to ignite, and I couldn't help but smile at the warmth radiating from his touch. "Please tell me that we can start again."

Suddenly, his strong arms enveloped me, pulling me against his warm body. Our eyes locked, and his finger traced a gentle line down my cheekbone. Every beat of my heart echoed his name, and as I held his gaze, I opened myself up completely, baring my soul to him in the hopes that he could see how much he meant to me.

"I guess I shouldn't be too surprised you're here," he said, his voice teasing and his lips curving into a cheeky grin. "I am pretty irresistible."

I gave him a playful slap on the arm, both of us laughing as the tension dissipated like mist in the morning sun. We remained in each other's arms, lost in the moment, neither of us needing words to express the joy over our togetherness.

I was so lost in his presence that I almost forgot about the cake. Breaking free from his embrace, I took his hands in mine and faced him. "So, since we're starting over, why don't we begin by baking another cake."

His surprised expression nearly had me laughing. "A cake? Sure. If that's what you want. Who's it for?"

"Does the name Celeste Deborough sound familiar?" I said, watching for his reaction.

At first, his eyebrows furrowed in confusion. "Who is Celes—wait a second, you don't mean—"

"If you're referring to the socialite, gallery owner, and heir to the Deborough fortune, then yes, I do."

He shook his head, clearing the shock from his face. "Why on earth would we make her a cake?"

"Connections. An artist friend of mine is her boyfriend, and he asked us to make Celeste a cake for her thirtieth birthday party."

"Are you kidding?" he asked, picking me up and spinning me around, excitement bubbling between us. "This is ridiculous. Yes, yes, let's do it."

"All right, partner," I said. "Let's shake on it."

Instead of shaking my hand, he drew me in for a kiss—and what a kiss! It was the perfect blend of love and laughter, of passion and joy. It was a promise and the first step toward a bright future with shared adventures.

Best of all, it was home.

# Epilogue

GUNNER AND I BEGAN our jog, our feet pounding against the pavement as we made our way through the city. By the time we reached the top of Mount Royal, our breaths were heavier than usual, as we hadn't been jogging since Lucy's arrival. But we made our way to our spot, and I stared out over the city, the skyline shimmering like a field of earthly stars.

As the wind picked up around us, I called out into the night. "Thank you, Daniel. Because of you, I know love and am ready to love again. You will always be in my heart, and I will always love you, but the time has come for me to move on." Then I kneeled down and kissed the palm of my hand before placing it on our engraving, tracing the letters with a finger. V + D. "Goodbye."

For a moment, I remained still, taking in the sounds of the city at night as my words traveled into the ether.

Gunner sighed, looked at me, the engraving, then at me again. I gave him a kiss on the top of his head. "It's time to go."

He barked and wagged his tail, and then we headed home, guided by the twinkling lights of the city and by love—both old and new.

# About Janet Koops

Janet Koops is a Canadian living in Colorado. A former librarian, Janet is a happily married empty-nester who writes full-time from her home just east of the Rocky Mountains. When she is not writing, she can typically be found hiking with her Alaskan Husky or working on a DIY reno project. Janet is a hopeless romantic who loves writing about complex women, their emotional journeys, and the healing power of love. For updates, new release notifications, and more, please visit janetkoops.com.

### Connect with Janet!

www.janetkoops.com
Goodreads: janetkoops
BookBub: @janetkoops1
Instagram: @janetkoops
Pinterest: Author Janet Koops
janet@janetkoops.com

### For a complete list of Janet's books, please visit

https://janetkoops.com